Bill Ripley is a native of Mason, Texas. [This is his first] novel.

BILL RIPLEY

Prisoners

PALADIN
GRAFTON BOOKS
A Division of the Collins Publishing Group

LONDON GLASGOW
TORONTO SYDNEY AUCKLAND

Paladin
Grafton Books
A Division of the Collins Publishing Group
8 Grafton Street, London W1X 3LA

A Paladin UK Original 1989

ISBN 0-586-08764-8

Printed and bound in Great Britain by
Collins, Glasgow

Set in Melior

This book is dedicated to Alice and Fisher Alsup

Acknowledgments

Poppy, Momma Ruth, Dolly Mommy, Fisher, Fooshie, Fido and Carl Jr took care of me early and stuck by me living or dead. The Barbados Sex Slave lent me his cave. My sons Brandon and Jerry and their mother Katherine gave me a hold on the earth. Vicky, Anny, Sharon and my sisters, Theresa and Lisa, probably saved my life. John and Billy Don were kind enough not to kill me. Afghan Huck, Hickenlooper, Neel, Billy Bob, John Howard and John Russel helped me over some hard times and demonstrated what it is to be a man of honor. Les Standiford, Jim Crumley and Dagoberto Molino Gilb lent me strength. John Dick, Freeman and Lyle Nordin unfortunately got me jobs. Christian Lund provided a moment of clarity and The Rat screamed in it. Carol Geane, Phyllis Hyland, Yvonne Golston, Mary Jane, Mike Norton, Zimmer, Steinmetz, Pee Wee, Wynn Cooper, Larry Levis, Harmonica Barry, Bradley, Jerry Williams and Andy Fishback could make me laugh in the middle of a shit storm. Fred Hill kept me out of the cold. Teb Obrien invented winky. Slow Bites took acid in the bathtub and Uncle Temptation, the venerable Stanley Cannon, renewed a sense of gentility. Carmen and Otto Milleti and Patricia Montgomery bought me a drink when I needed it. Jeff, Cindy and little Bubby let me use the phone and pain pills. Michael Holden helped create little Bill and Annie, which was nice, but he also gave me some Bum Phillips cowboy boots in very poor taste. Rust Hills showed Gary 'The Monster.' Gary must be a genius. This is just the tip of the iceberg. There is passion, grace, luck, courage and pleasant insanity everywhere. And without the love and support of Ellen Elizabeth Everett, her poetry of mind and soul, and her great big strong loving heart, you wouldn't be holding this book in your hands.

Well, I won't have to chop no wood
I can be bad or I can be good

– Emmylou Harris,
'*One of These Days*'

1

It is getting increasingly difficult to have a little fun without ticking somebody off. Either you're spending their money or fiddling with their wives or, bingo, you do too much coke and can't get it up with a Yugoslav gymnast who looks like Geraldine Chaplin. Something is amiss, thinks Danny Devoto as he crosses the Sunset Strip, wishing he were back in Buffalo eating black snow. Something is out of whack.

In a few minutes the Los Angeles smog will redden, and the Strip will squirm awake. By then he wants to be in his apartment, in bed with Mindy, in bed with his milk shake. He's giving up. He wants to turn into oatmeal. Truncate the sex drive; stem the restlessness; pull off the highway – become oatmeal. He stops on the second landing and takes a gulp of strawberry shake and, over his shoulder, watches a normal person squeeze from the musky hallway onto the red sidewalk.

Inside his apartment, he sits on the bed and lets Mindy chew on his ankles. She's the only small dog he's ever liked. A Yorkshire terrier. He wishes he had a big red convertible to ride her around in. They could drive up the coast together. But that would not be oatmeal. Oatmeal lies down on its bed and looks at the Sheetrock up on the ceiling. Danny wonders who Sheetrocked this place. Probably drank beer. Had babies. No red convertible for that guy. But then again, no red convertible for Danny either. Poverty, the wages of restlessness. He tries not to think about dying. His body has aged, yet at thirty-seven he's still at the end of an extended adolescence, shooting for early senility, hoping to skip everything in between. He thinks about his grandmother, whose house smelled like old china, musty shawls, German junk. The smell of responsibility.

Enough to drive one into the nice, nasty streets.

Money's been a problem ever since a linebacker crushed Hugo's left knee just as he'd nailed down a full ride to Oklahoma. That's when the tomato started to rot. And some days the whole ceiling of the health club reddens as he strains to recall a patch of blue sky he'd glimpsed over his shoulder one bright afternoon as he turned to catch a lovely pass for a touchdown. He'd sort of floated across the goal line. In that blue sky was promise, glory. But it ain't there anymore.

He sells Yellow Page ads across West Texas. On the road he misses Hugo, Jr, and worries about his wife, who once needed a lot of hosing yet recently joined a group to get more independent. Her eyes are hard. She doesn't come fishing with him and little Hugo these days, and Hugo worries that he's been making women his slaves. Lifting weights only helps so much, and afterward he wants to punch something, which is not nice. Last week he put his fist through the couch and needed stitches, little Hugo crying in the hot emergency room.

In bed, Mary Ann reads a magazine while he thinks about the tomato of his death. There it is as always, just about to rot. Sometimes he can feel it dripping on him. Tonight he tries to cheer himself by thinking maybe little Hugo won't have a tomato. Maybe he won't get his knees hurt. Maybe that bright blue panhandle sky will spiral open into an endless circle of joy.

* * *

It was back when Gregorian chants and candlelight and incense were the traditional accoutrements, back before Danny realized that he hallucinated a lot better in a dark room alone. Later on, his place became the bathtub. He took his clothes off and lay down inside the cool porcelain without running any water, in absolute darkness, and after a few hours the word *highways* took on new meanings. But that was later. The night they locked the cats in the bathroom, they were trying to get rid of distractions.

A spiritual trip. A purity trip. Good acid. An attempted clear-light experience that almost made it. Within the magnificent blinking walls, the crazy halls and wordless wonder of the inwardly expanding monstrous intimacy of the stars, they almost became at one with a pulsing white energy, except for a strange olfactory sensation that seemed to be peeking in and out of the edges of the universe, which gradually became pervasive, until, tinkling down through the constellations, it was a bad smell.

Death experience, Danny registered. Death most foul. God's way of immersing us in what we mistakenly consider the real world, which, He shows us, is *not* the way.

See, Kim?

What Kim and Danny finally saw were six poopcovered kittens streaking around the bathtub. Frantic blurbs. They'd forgotten to include the litter box with the kittens, and the little devils had fouled the tub, become hysterically entrapped in slimy porcelain. This was wormy, white-walled insanity. And talk about a bathtub ring.

'Gosh,' said Kim. 'Look at those puppies squirm.'

Lester was on his way to Peru, and though he didn't know exactly what he wanted to write, or even if he actually wanted to write, he had a vague desire to make people give up greed, play more, diddle more, breed less, kill less, etc. These were the sixties.

Working in the nursing home, Les had been disturbed by paralyzed old George, a wealthy Baptist who had worked eighteen hours a day to get rich and denied himself almost every pleasure along the way. Now he was without friends. For ten years he'd lain trapped in his chicken skin, his brain a golf ball, his fortune useless.

The Lord works in strange ways, thought young Les as he looked over the top of his book, *Childhood and Society*, and down the aisle at the resigned, numb citizens of the richest country in the world. He realized it was hopeless. Nothing he had to say would be relevant until the money was redistributed and the population thinned out, so that people had time to think and feel instead of just slaving away.

And this, he felt, was not about to happen. The big guys who ran things didn't want you thinking or feeling. It slowed down production. They wanted you scared and working so you wouldn't bump up against the truth – life could be fun. Yup, they wanted you scared. They wanted you grim. They wanted you madly cranking out Barbie dolls and doorknobs and carburetors, or they wanted you selling Amway or Post Toasties or Xerox, or they wanted you overworked and underpaid at teaching so you could at least feel smart, and they wanted you to keep having kids so you'd have to keep working at whatever job you were stuck in and not have time to think or feel or, if you did, you certainly wouldn't have time to do anything about it, or even get close to the big fun, the fun that belonged only to them. And then they wanted your kids to hop onto the same treadmill.

Enough people were born every year so that thousands starved to death; the Pope made sure of it. And clever bankers arranged profitable wars using common folk for cannon fodder. But Lester would try. A lonely and noble effort would be made to write a Peruvian book so compelling, so devious, that mankind would be tricked into shedding the clichés and mind-numbing routines that enslaved it, would reforest and depopulate and put all the nasty technology underground. People would take time to explore their hearts and minds with the energy they wasted working in the factories of boredom and the shallow, mathematical repetition of banking and marketing. On top of that, he'd be famous, get lots of winky and wouldn't have to work in the nursing home.

He was excited; it seemed to him that travel was real, and he enjoyed staying awake as the bus flew across the night. As he was congratulating himself on quitting school and getting real, a girl and her baby sat down across the aisle. She wore a red, stained pantsuit and gave him a hurt look as she stuffed a bottle into the infant's mouth. She wasn't really fat, he reasoned. More like stocky, actually.

'Nice baby,' he said.

She turned the crushed look on him again, and he thought she might not speak. Then, as if she'd somehow decided he wasn't a pervert, she looked down into the baby's gobbling face. 'That's my little lover,' she said.

Flat miles drifted by, and a couple of times Lester caught her looking at him. Something about her was different. Finally he snapped the book shut, stretched noisily and checked.

'Where you from?' he asked.

'Wisconsin.' She looked wistful, then serious. 'Going back to Mama now, though.' She looked sadly at the child.

'Why you going to Tulsa?' He said it to sound like he couldn't believe a neat girl like her would live in Tulsa.

'I'm leaving my old man.' She looked at Les accusingly, then shifted the baby. 'You sure ask a lot of questions.'

Les shrugged.

Her eyes hardened. 'I'm a Baptist, ya know. My old man ran around with the boys all the time, never coming home. Never spending time with the baby. So I left him. Now me and the baby are going home. You got any gum?'

'No.'

She looked at him with disgust, then seemed to soften. 'Whatya reading?'

'A book.'

'Lemme see.'

Les handed her *Childhood and Society*, and she propped it up against the kid.

'This a book about raising kids?' She fanned the pages, twisted in her seat.

'Sort of. It's more theoretical, though. It says there are seven stages of development pretty much common to children everywhere.'

'You a college boy?'

She couldn't have meant that facetiously, he thought. 'I'm leaving college.'

'Yeah? Why?'

'I'm going to Peru.' Les felt ridiculous. You couldn't tell a girl like this you wanted to write, so he tried to sound rich. 'I've got to stop off at my uncle's ranch in Stillwater and say good-bye.'

Her eyes shone. She shifted the baby. 'What's your name?'

'Lester Darling.'

'I'm Jody Carlene May. Pleased to meet you.'

'Likewise. That's a pretty name.'

'Thank you. You can call me Jody. That ranch is in a real pretty part of Oklahoma.'

'Yeah. I like it.'

'Is is big?'

'Real big.'

'Then why you going to Peru?'

'Restless.'

'Uh-oh.'

'Why uh-oh?'

'My old man was restless, the baby's daddy. See where my wedding ring used to be?' She stuck her puffy hand across the aisle, and Lester held it as long as he thought he could. It was a long time.

'Yeah, he was always going out and getting drunk with the boys and never paying no attention to the baby. It ain't right. And it's specially hard being a Baptist.'

What was it about this girl anyway, he wondered, getting hard himself. She had magnetism.

'Why does that make it any harder?'

'All that drinking and running around is against our religion. You know that.' She looked into his eyes and pulled her hand away. As she brushed the baby's sparse hair off its forehead, Les felt he should explain to her about religion.

'But sometimes you just can't help it.' She sighed, looking out the window. 'Like that boy who got on the bus in Omaha. He just kept kissing me and kissing me. Then we had a little beer the in back of the bus. He sure was persistent.'

There was a pint of vodka in his suitcase, Les realized as he started in. 'I think religion is basically bad. Jesus may have been okay, but the Church turned his trip into a con. It's a trick. Look at all the wars it's started. People don't need religion to decide if they're being nice to each other. You have to feel that stuff. More often, people use the rules of religion to be mean to each other, hide from the truth and make money. It's cheap. I don't mean you're cheap, of course.'

'What about the Golden Rule?'

'What if I'm a masochist?'

'A what?'

'Somebody who likes to be tortured.'

She seemed awed. 'Why, then you'd have to torture everybody.'

'Right. How would you like that?'

She seemed to think on it. 'You're a strange person. It seems like you think a lot.'

The baby was asleep, and Les leaned over to look into its fat, wrinkled face. 'It sure is a cute baby,' he said.

'He's my little lover.' Her breath was warm on his ear. 'For a minute I didn't like you, but if you like babies, you can't be all bad.'

Lester tried to control himself, tried to shut up about religion and pull himself away from her. She was obviously in heat. On the verge of trembling, he settled slowly back into his seat and pretended to read.

The bus thundered along. Headlights blossomed and passed.

'Hey, Les?'

'Yeah.'

'Would you do me a favor?'

'Sure, Jody. What's that?'

'Could I lay the baby over there so he can have two seats? I don't get many chances to put him down. . . . You could sit over here.'

'Sure.' He was almost embarrassed by how easily it was working out.

Padding the seats with his coat, he lifted the baby, praying it wouldn't wake up.

'There,' she said. 'I hope the little devil sleeps a while.'

She leaned back and looked into the rolling night, their reflections hurtling over the earth. Then they were looking into the reflections of each other's eyes, her features soft in the dark glass.

Layered realities, he thought.

18

'I think you're real honest,' she whispered.

'That's *my* religion.'

'Les?'

'Yes.'

'Do you ever do that stuff? Kissing and everything?'

'Sometimes. I think it's good for you. It keeps you from repressing things.' He looked up at the luggage rack and tried to seem far away, lost in thought.

Outside, the flatlands broke and some hills cropped up. A man up front coughed.

'You're a strange person, Lester.'

'No I'm not.'

'Yes you are.'

'Why?'

'Because you think so much.'

'Oh.'

'I think you're okay . . . I don't care what they think.'

She leaned her head on his shoulder as he wondered who *they* were. Soon he was kissing her, and her hand found his unit. She covered them with her coat.

He was inside her. 'Come, dammit. Come deeper,' she hissed.

Les tried to hold her so she wouldn't kick the seat in front. It was difficult, though they were turned like spoons toward the window. She grew exasperated.

'God. I've got to have you. Come with me to Tulsa.'

'What about your mother?'

'Piss on her.'

He'd never heard a girl talk about her mother like that. He came, feeling sort of guilty about seducing a poor dumb Baptist with a fatherless baby. But she wouldn't let him pull out. They rode along in silence while he firmed up an excuse for going on alone to Stillwater. He'd say his aunt was dying.

19

The baby cried.

'Here. Take this.' Jody handed him a bottle without turning around, without dislodging him. 'Put that in his mouth.'

He reached the bottle across the aisle with his free arm, blindly seeking the baby's mouth. Soon it was quiet. A soft slurping filled the silence, and he realized that everyone on the bus had heard them. But he couldn't move. Jody held him tightly, and if he let the bottle go, it would fall and the baby would cry. Up the aisle, a woman looked over her shoulder at him and shook her head.

'Les?'

'Yes?' He looked at the luggage rack, trying again to seem far away and lost in thought.

'I lied to you about something.'

'Well, we all tell little lies now and then, Jody.' He relaxed, happy she'd lied to him. 'The main thing is to work toward the truth.'

'I'm not really a Baptist, Les.'

'Well, you know how I feel about religion. That's okay. Why'd you lie in the first place?' Suddenly he wasn't feeling so guilty anymore, but his arm was tired of holding the bottle.

'My old man's in a motorcycle gang called the Machitos. You never know what strangers will think about that, so I always tell 'em I'm a Baptist. It's safer.'

'A motorcycle gang?'

Life magazine had just done a feature on the Hell's Angels, and that's all Les knew about motorcycle gangs. In general he felt about gangs like he did about religion. Same junk.

'I don't like gangs.'

'Me neither, no more.'

'Why?'

'My old man made me poke all those guys. And then,

20

when he'd sober up, he'd get jealous. Had me poke guys from the Bimbos too. Both holes. Then, when I did it once by myself, he got mad and kicked me out. That wasn't very nice, was it?'

Lester's erection made like a Brussels sprout. 'Nope,' he admitted.

He twisted away from her, as though to check on the baby. The bottle was empty. The child was fast asleep. It was an ugly baby. When his arm was free, he pulled up his pants, wondering how many cases of clap he'd just caught.

She wrapped her arms around him and gave him a long, deep kiss. 'You're different, Les,' she said, 'you're very understanding. Would you bring me some toilet paper?'

He remembered penicillin in his overnight bag and took it with him to the rest room; there was also aftershave lotion that was mostly alcohol. He swallowed pills, poured shaving lotion over his shriveled unit, which seemed to be trying to crawl inside him, and doubled up in pain as alcohol seeped into the opening.

When he got back, Jody was staring at her hand, opening and closing the fingers, which were webbed with semen.

'You were gone a long time. There's come all over the seat.'

'Shh.'

'What's that smell?'

'Nothing.'

The bus smelled like a barbershop, and after he sat back down, she snuggled up against him.

'You spill your shaving lotion, silly?'

He stared at the luggage rack, for some reason thinking about George, lying paralyzed in his bed in the nursing home. Les also felt trapped, like he'd rather sit up front. But if George could lie in the same bed for ten years, Les could sit in the same seat until Tulsa. He could be nice without religion. He relaxed when she started to snore, but he had to stare down the woman up front, who was looking at him again.

2

Pecan tree, he dreams. White-hot sky and boiling noon shade. Sprinklers arching silver circles onto the green, terraced lawn. Danny's four years old, in a pecan tree waiting for his grandfather to rattle home in his pickup. Up on the screen porch, beneath the ceiling fan, beneath his grandmother's age-splotched hands, a lunch of cold salmon and shoestring potatoes appears on the circular table. Locusts saw the still, hot air in this small town, and sometimes a diesel drones down the endless highway.

Then he's falling.

The door to his shabby apartment is whamming like his heart. When he lurches awake and slips the latch, Wendy McDougall – chubby heiress to a sandwich-bag fortune and writer of blowsy poetry – falls through the door drunk, pounding away on the floor. She's blubbering about life.

This girl is in need of solace, Danny thinks, tucking the pistol into a drawer. What about a quick cocktail down the road? Is that wrong? To help a friend? A Jack Daniel's. She grows interested in the boomerang shapes on the linoleum. Danny goes to the sink and tries to wash the milk shake off his tattered Hawaiian shirt. He likes Wendy, the blue eyes, the softness, like a golden retriever among dobermans here in 1985 Los Angeles. Just lift this sweet girl off the floor and ease the keys out of her purse.

'There, there. I'll drive.'

And then the palms are flicking by in the heavy evening, and though the car is not red, it *is* a convertible – a yellow Mustang with Mindy the terrier sitting atop the inert Miss McDougall in the backseat, the odd Yorkshire ears flooshing in the wind. Danny heads up the coast with the smell of horse sweat, sun, dust and cowshit somehow mingling with the Pacific wind's odor of eucalyptus, salt and asphalt, and he discovers the Mustang is fast. Twenty miles out of Santa Barbara he's doing a hundred and ten with one hand on the wheel, the other encouraging the Jack Daniel's out of its beautiful bottle. The ice melts. The moon pops up.

'Drive me to Dallas, Danny,' she mutters – and he remembers being under the Manhattan Beach pier when he'd had one of those perpetual stiffies brought on by one of those equally rare, perfect combinations of whiskey and cocaine; he'd brought her repeatedly to the point of orgasm, then held off till she whimpered and thrashed and begged him to make her come; but he'd refused until, out of some quirk, he'd insisted, 'Say, "Drive me to Dallas."' And she did.

But the real Dallas disgusts him. Next time he'd make her say Waxahachie, Nacogdoches, Turkey or Oatmeal. That's it: Oatmeal.

Drive me to Oatmeal, Danny.

A bit out of Austin up toward London, at the corner of Farm to Market Road 8579 and Highway 87, lies Oatmeal, home of the Oatmeal Cowboys, onetime single-A high-school football champions and two-time state champions in girls' basketball. There's a stone courthouse surrounded by the drug and feed stores, the Oatmeal National Bank, lumberyard, saddle and gun shop and a grocery. Interspersed between these buildings are vacant lots, connected to the dry, creaking vastness of West Texas by dry, creaking vastness. On the courthouse lawn are some pecan trees, and under these pecan trees is a never-ending game of dominoes.

'Drive me to Dallas, Danny,' whispers Miss McDougall, and the Mustang swells with the love of speed and darkness. Why not? he reasons. Maybe by way of Las Vegas. Just get out of California for a while. Head south. When you answer the door with a pistol, it's time to take a break. Bingo. And not really Dallas. In that direction. Drift around a bit. The faces of his white-haired aunts in the choir of the Oatmeal First Christian Church flash before him as the Mustang finds its way to I-15. Danny figures they'll bankroll themselves in Nevada, at the blackjack tables. At dawn he slices across the gravel parking lot of Ned's Truck Stop and is back with doughnuts, beer, milk and coffee as Wendy sits up, rubbing her eyes.

'Where are we?'

'Almost Dallas.'

She smiles. 'That's not what I meant by "Drive me to Dallas".'

'Next stop, Las Vegas.'

It's good to stretch his legs, and the sun frizzles the back of his neck as she drifts toward the rest room, pepping up just before she disappears behind the WOMEN. Women, he thinks. How nice for her, waking to the rhythm of the road. My decision. She's innocent. He thinks she wants babies and old age – like Christine. By the time she slides across the seat and kisses him good morning, he feels trapped.

He splatters a beaten VW with gravel as he burns out of the truck stop, melancholy at the startled, ancient hippie faces behind the windshield. They give him the finger as he envisions his life as Wendy's husband – heir to a sandwich-bag fortune. He'd be bored in a year. He pops a Budweiser as an eighteen-wheeler almost blows him into six jack-rabbits, and he remembers he's in Nevada – no speed limit.

She versifies:

O zipper zap
I took a nap
Upon that fateful day.

For Danny Devoto
The incompetent loádo
Had taken me out to play

Through the desert we rode
Like two horny toads
Getting in each other's way.

In Las Vegas they lose a lot of money. What he remembers, as Wendy lifts his head to place beneath it another pillow, is the neon splash on the blackjack table and cowboy boots. People were kicking him. This doesn't matter. What matters is sheets like new hundred-dollar bills, and she is elevating his head, pillow by pillow, until he is able to sip orange juice. After he swallows, she changes the washcloth.

The dog is watching television. Life is nice with the dark drapes drawn. He dreams of a windmill. It is summer; he is eight years old and has walked across three backyards to eat some of Miss Emmy's sugar bread and fool around with the goats the old Germans keep. Beyond the fence is endless mesquite and endless cactus, and every ten or fifteen miles is a dry, granite-bottomed creek. The windmill rises from a blistered clapboard pump house into air that burns lungs. Very seldom, maybe twice a day, a breeze nudges the vane on the windmill, and the pump rod creaks in its casing, and the chickens lift their heads in frozen expectation.

That is the sound of his childhood.

The sound that wakes him is the sound of bedsprings from the next bed. The sandwich-bag heiress indeed meant 'Drive me to Dallas' metaphorically. She seems to be strangling in a paroxysm of masturbation while dreaming about iguanas. He thinks he should perhaps do something. He tries to sit up as she twists on her back and doesn't look too plump at all. Her shirt falls open, nipples blipping, and her little heels dig into the mattress and her hips lift off the bed. Danny wonders what she's dreaming. It's not fair. She exhales, trembling, and the vision of a taller man entwined in her babyish embrace makes him jealous, yet he has an erection. She grows still. Oatmeal, he reminds himself, getting hold of himself. Think about Oatmeal.

Before the hills of Oatmeal there's the quiet, cypress- and adobe-filled valleys of northern New Mexico. In the sixties they were full of hippies and artsy types. Rich and poor aesthetes alike. VW buses. Zoom. Zoom. Zoom. The yellow Mustang shoots through Cortez, Durango, Chama, Taos and takes the back road over the mountains of Ojo Sarco and through Penasco until suddenly there yawns before them the pastel expanse of the Santa Fe basin. The Sangre de Cristos soar behind as they thump across the ruined asphalt into the tiny town of Truchas, which hangs nine thousand feet up on the side of the peak, wood smoke rising from tilting mud hovels.

Danny lived here once. Chopped wood. Sat around the wood stove. Smoked pot. Zoom. Zoom. Zoom. Down the mountain. Into Pojoaque with the odd wooden fences like laced spears made of cedar and then flash through the phony turquoise town of Santa Fe and, bam, they're finally closing in on Muleshoe, Texas, one of the lonelier, more desolate places – a hard, flat version of infinity. It's for getting out of, for driving through.

He remembers the summers before air conditioners when they kept a bucket of ice on the floor by the vents and he and his little sister dampened towels and draped them over their necks and whined as they Ping-Ponged between Denver and Oatmeal, through the red dust and fence posts, while his war-widowed mother slapped together a TV career and longed sadly for her father, the big gentle German Danny

27

had grown up with beneath pecan trees. And here he is, driving through it again, with a Yorkshire terrier that looks like a miniature lion, and he wonders how this little dog would survive in the back of an old GMC pickup, tiny feet reaching toward the rifle rack, trying to balance as they bump-bump across rutted pasture in blue dusk. It's just not Fido.

Fido had been a big, slow black Labrador. Deliberate. Tough. Unperturbed. Nobody fucked with Danny when Fido was there. As far back as his memory went, Danny remembers lying under the lilac bush curled up in the dust around Fido. But this Yorkshire terrier. An old lady's dog. A fag dog. Danny had awakened in an alley in West LA one night, behind some garbage cans, with an odd, rough tongue and cold nose searching his bruised face. The thing looked like a drug-addled rat silhouetted against what seemed a fireworks display but was in fact a couple of artists entertaining themselves by soaking a litter of Yorkshire terriers in kerosene, snipping their feet off with bolt cutters and lighting them on fire.

And now he's taking her to Texas.

Fence posts flying.

Boredom, Lester thinks. Life goes on – on the surface. Intellectuals and sales managers weave nets. We wear blinders. We get religion. We get ahead. We get cornflakes. We get head. We get knowledge. We get laid. Then we get Appalachia. We get the ghetto. We getty up and go. Formula, he thinks, is the key. Formula. Tedium. Sales. Somehow corporate America has sold us the idea that success is the hourly death of acquisitive ass-kissing slavery. You know. Progress.

He looks out over Houston from his office. The telephone company has been good to him. It has let him merge with the faceless. He's come in from the storms. There's comfort in insulation. No more direct contact with the madness. He stands back now and manipulates quietly. Most of the fear and anger is gone, he hopes, most of the driving pain. He has risen. He is detached. Life is like chess.

He buzzes his secretary and asks her to view a training video with him. It's a boring video: A neatly groomed executive is pointing to a chart. Lester asks his secretary to take notes. Watches her try to concentrate. The video lecture is as dull as the executive is lifeless, but she begins to twist in her seat, casting sidelong looks at Lester. He has never touched or encouraged her, but she is suddenly sexually aroused and having trouble sitting still. Her plain face blushes as she tries to concentrate on note taking. She has always been prudish, detached, but now her tongue flicks across her upper lip. Her eyes fix on the video and she gasps, begins to tremble.

He smiles.

Dumb as dirt, thinks Lester, watching Hugo cross the lobby. Hugo's smiling like an ostrich. Hugo's big, serene face is strangely lit with happiness today, and he does a short, soft-shoe shuffle before the revolving glass door, dancing to secret music. Lester's surprised how light on his feet the big guy is – a giant Tweety bird or Baby Huey. A numb-nuts. But perfect to cover for Lester while he's taking care of a bothersome turn of events.

Sure, the whole thing's a little out of hand, perhaps a titch of death, but no hill for a stepper. And especially for one with a sense of humor. Do I have humor, smiles Lester.

Lester had befriended Rudy Archuleta in the oil fields during a college summer job. Being a sensitive sort and knowing he was middle-class, Lester felt it important to get in good with salt-of-the-earth types like Rudy. They made his spirit feel bigger, and even back then, he knew they might be useful.

After the Tet Offensive he quit caring about having a bigger spirit, but when he got back from Vietnam, he eventually looked up Rudy and realized he might be useful. He always stopped in at Archuleta's trailer, and Lucy and Rudy and the six rug rats were glad to have him for a buddy.

'Lester the Molester,' Rudy called him, after they started honky-tonking, theoretically on fishing trips. And:

'What's better than Lester?'

'More Lester! Molester!'

'Yar. Yar. Yar.'

Rudy Archuleta was a giant, and Lester was not afraid in bars. It was nice to get out of his suit, wear cowboy boots and a work shirt, and drink a long-neck Lone Stars and shoot pool. Emanating a cosmopolitan slickness that confused and attracted the city-hungry cowgirls, Lester was never long out of the saddle. Back in Houston, he'd turn intellectual, make with feminist jive, keep himself in twitchy college girls. He worked hard and had good intuition, which had failed him with Richard Longley, but that was fixed now, or almost.

When Lester had first sensed trouble, he took Richard on a couple of weekend romps with Rudy. When he was convinced Richard was going to betray the video scam, he got Rudy to think Richard had been diddling Lucy, Rudy's wife. He even drew a crude picture of it on the toilet stall, in the bathroom of the Lonesome Duck, Rudy's favorite bar.

Easy as that.

'He took awhile to die.' Rudy laughed over the phone, his voice an octave high and goofy-hysterical. *'Un ratito.'*

Lester had it on tape. Jealousy was bad.

3

In the darkness of the sleeping bag, Danny is amazed at the tightness of Wendy's squeaky winky. It is so tight, he feels like a monster.

'Oooo. Oooo. Oooo. Oooo. Oooo,' she chirps.

'Wee wee. Wee wee.'

'Wee.'

The shell inside his mind breaks forth, spilling lizards of sensation. He is the jungle, the lake's edge.

'That was a hell of an orgasm.'

'Wee.'

They began animal sex roles in Amarillo. They did the hummingbird, the frog. The cat-and-dog combo was nice and quick. Expanded the personality.

'Wee wee.'

'Woof woof.'

'Grr.'

Tapped deep Jungian reservoirs.

'I felt close to stars and worms and wings, Danny. I forgot everything.'

'Woof.'

'Slither.'

'Peep.'

'I'm drowning.' She gurgles as a wave splashes Danny's neck. They have squirmed out of his sleeping bag and squiggled through the mud till they are half in a small, misty lake. It is dawn. Birds sing.

The next wave splashes their faces.

He is oddly excited about building a fire, anticipates odors, feels the earth stretch. Cedars line the shore. Soft silence. Why did I ever leave? He can't even hear a plane.

'Gravy.'

'Biscuits.' He touches breasts.

'Jam.' He pulls away, begins to gather kindling. Food sex, he thinks. Lemon meringue pie. Big Sister could eat a whole one. He tries to imagine his grandparents making whoopee. Sex is beautiful if you love each other, Big said, otherwise you're like animals.

'Weef. Weef,' Wendy calls, pointing at a body in the lake.

It is bloated and floating fifteen feet from the shore. A snake curls on the white flesh in the sun. So much for breakfast. So much for last night's Whataburger, which blossoms from Wendy's pretty mouth upon the camp fire. A leg is missing from the jellied corpse, and water worms writhe in hollows that once were eyes. Danny feels his own Whataburger bolting but fights it down, forces himself to look into a clump of cactus where bees hover by bright yellow flowers. Though he thinks of stagecoaches and Japanese prints, the wind changes and he retches.

'Welcome to Dallas,' he whispers when they are several miles down the asphalt. Tire prints would be in the mud by the lake. Someone might have seen the Mustang. Why no leg? Something like this could interrupt a nice little escape.

'We left our sleeping bags.'

'Too bad,' he says, floors it, heads south.

'What if that was your father?'

Forget this corpse, Danny tells himself. Just forget it. Naturally it's a sign from God. Ignore it. Do I call the cops when a school bus burns in Beirut? But there's a difference. God's burning children on TV. Something is amiss, thinks Danny Devoto. Something is out of whack. What if it was my father? What indeed? They never found *my* father. And who'd want to be remembered as a sea-bloated corpse? He went down with the plane. Flesh peeling like cooked fish.

'Look, Danny, we should *tell* somebody.'

'Forget that.'

'It's my car.'

She's got a point there. They're also her credit cards. We didn't exactly strike it rich in Vegas. Smalltown cops make him nervous – they don't have enough to do. They don't love him. They don't. But what has he done bad recently? He's not worked.

'Okay.' He sighs. 'But say we live off your money.'

'What's new?'

The corpse has floated under some brush at the pond's edge, and one of its arms rips off in Deputy Welch's hands. This seems to worsen his mood. Wendy sits under a cedar tree with a handkerchief pressed against her face, holding the suddenly hysterical dog. What a great morning, thinks Danny, what a blessed day. The police radio squeaks, and he feels sick. No luggage. Calm down. You've just brushed the heat. Remember, you're not vagrant. You're clean. You're a sandwich-bag baron.

'Get that bag over here.'

Sergeant Ramirez is on the radio, and Danny hands Welch the body bag. As he moves back through the brush he sees a small plastic case, which he might pass off as a shaving kit. He palms it and moves to Wendy, has her slip it in her purse.

'Put my new razors and toothbrush in that.'

'That'll fool 'em.'

He sits by Wendy, trying not to throw up. Sleeping bags. A shaving kit. That's fairly stable.

'Gopher shit,' groans Sergeant Ramirez. He looks at a

series of holes in the corpse's forehead, then walks away from the jellied heap and stares up at a dove's nest and lowers a branch to peek inside.

Danny asks, 'Can we go?'

'Yeah, we verified the girl's story. But it sounds like you oughta get a job.'

'We've got money.'

'She's got money.'

'I've got money.' Wendy laughs when they're back on the road. 'Boy, don't I have money.'

Danny is shaking. Wendy is talking about money, and he's thinking about handcuffs. He opens his mouth and lets the cedar-rich air fill his lungs. He's going back. The hills are close and familiar. He is a child again, back when God sits over to the left of the windmill and just a little bit higher. When that rare breeze turns the blades in the god-awful August heat, the screech of the plunging rod causes the chickens to jerk their heads skyward, and even the goats to look up into the bright, empty sky. This is where Danny got his fill of God, in the brutal, dead West Texas afternoon. God up there behind the buzzards turning the mesquite beans yellow and watching him jerk off. God hovering over the courthouse, watching old men hunched over dominoes in the shade. God designing each splash of tobacco, remembering each snakebite.

Training a beagle pup to hunt, young Danny tries to wound a jackrabbit so the dog will have a trace of blood to trail. But the bullet opens up the mother's belly, and out drop six baby rabbits, all softly linked by placenta, all dragged through the rock and cactus as the mother miraculously thrashes and lunges ahead of the dog, who finally latches on to the hindmost fetus, somersaulting her forward in a pinwheel of blood. God of Easter. God of new bluebonnets shimmering down the bar ditches of the two-lane blacktop into the heat-shimmered asphalt of Abilene, Sweet-water, Lubbock and points so far north and flat that the skin of the brain cracks . . .

God's everywhere. In banks. Not just in rock churches. In Dallas. Under Danny's pillow. At football games. He tells Danny's grandma that He gave His only Son and that He Himself was at the Alamo.

His grandma teaches him to read before first grade. She teaches him to swim, even though she can't. Teaches him to wash dishes, mow the lawn, talk to God, shake hands, wipe himself and catch a baseball. The town calls her Big Sister, or just Big.

But halfway to the filling station he's forgotten about Big. He's across the cactus-choked lot that separates the high school from the highway, and an eighteen-wheeler is upshifting just beyond the Dairy Queen, heading out of town, and all that menopausal warbling in church is like so much static to the whine of the diesel as it blows out of sight.

And that's the highway. That's where he lives.

Lester stands in the doorway of Rudy's big pink trailer and looks at Lucy's bruised and hysterical face. Her jaws are wired shut from when Rudy beat her up, and the kids are bawling, so Les has trouble understanding her. Finally he makes out that Rudy is at the Lonesome Duck, still pretty mad, thinks he'll be executed. The squalling children make Lester consider fertility drugs for Ethiopia; maybe send the Pope down, the old breed-'em-till-they-starve trick. Now that's entertainment.

Lucy's sick with fright. Kids cry. It's hot. He's starting to understand the clenched and frantic groanings.

'What made him think this?' She trembles. Her eyes fill with tears. 'That I would sleep with someone?'

'It's written in the bathroom at the bar. He was drunk. You know how he gets.'

'He's crazy.'

'I know.' Lester gives her a hug. 'I'll help. Maybe nothing will happen.'

'*Tien cuidado.*'

'*Y tu.*'

Kids cry.

On the way to the bar, Lester thinks maybe starvation *is* the answer. A nice, slow, ugly death. Obviously the Pope had a sense of humor. Forty thousand babies a day starve to gut-wrenching death, but he has a nice house and gets to travel, spreading the Word: Have faith, make babies. Eat dirt. Now there's a salesman, a heartbreaker.

'Let's get out of here, Rudy.'

'*Amigo.*'

'I've got a bottle in the car.'

They drive out a dirt road slowly, swapping shots of Old Crow. Lester drinks little, blocking the mouth with his tongue, as he studies Rudy. Jealousy, how quaint.

'You need to calm down. He deserved it.'

Rudy drinks. 'I cut off his leg. I don't know why.'

'Even if he didn't squeegee her, he still deserved it.' Lester watches this register on the big man's face. 'What did you do with his stuff?'

'Didn't squeegee her?'

'He's queer, Rudy.'

'But I thought – '

'I know what you thought. We were just considering the possibility, man, because some joker wrote it on the bathroom wall. An old joke. I didn't know you were taking it seriously.'

'Oh, Lester, I am an idiot.' Whiskey bubbles from Rudy's nose. 'A bad person.'

* * *

Rudy hunkers in the shade of a scrub oak. The bottle of Old Crow is nearly empty. Lester puts it to his own lips and again does not drink. Sweat drops from his chin as he looks into the sunset. It seems Rudy tossed Richard's stuff all over the place. Lester imagines Richard's frightened eyes when Rudy grabbed his briefcase.

'I felt the ice pick pop through his skull. I wiggled his brain. You should've seen his eyes.'

'He was a brainy guy.'

'A bad person?'

Lester hesitates.

'He wasn't a bad person?' Big tears well in Rudy's eyes. 'Was he okay, Lester?'

'He was a sneak.'

'But not a bad person?'

'Yes. Bad.'

'Good.'

Lester asks himself, Was Richard a bad person?

'He was so bad, man.' Rudy passes out against the tree, and Lester pulls the bottle from Rudy's hand and this time takes a real swallow. Was Richard a bad person? He imagines Richard's spiteful eyes twitching as the ice pick probed, and remembers Richard's eyes laughing when they came up with Sweet People Productions – a small company that made moral self-help videos. When the actors were finished, the videos completed, Lester sent the tapes to Richard, who somehow tracked, beneath the original, a bit of subliminal eroticism or violence. It was quite a technique. And nothing too heavy, except for special occasions, like his secretary. Just subtle tingles beneath anti-drug, pro-God videos. Work-ethic stuff, yet everybody goes home excited. Good for Kiwanis Clubs and church groups. And just for fun – rich white girls stroking impoverished Mexicans beneath migrant-labor videos.

* * *

Rudy feels weak, almost like he's not there. If it weren't for Lester, he thinks, he might kill himself. Hurt himself worse than he'd hurt Richard. It makes him sick to think what he did. He can still feel the ice pick twitch. He feels like throwing up, like he can't take care of himself. But Les reminds him that he must be strong – that his kids need him.

Les wants to see the place where he killed Richard. For some reason Les thinks he'll be able to help. It's confusing. They must check to see if he left any evidence. He wasn't very careful, but the thought of going back to the lake makes him feel cold.

God wouldn't have let this happen for no reason, right? This makes him feel better. That's right, God had a hand in it. God knew that innocent babies breathed the air that Richard breathed into after he slurped peckers that had poked poopers, so God wrote on the bathroom wall that Richard poked Lucy so Rudy would kill him. That's it. Richard was probably even thinking about little Tony . . .

Lester looks over Oatmeal, a quaint, Dutch number like most of these hill-country towns. Lester likes to call Germans 'Dutch' for the abuse of it. Also, it's just one syllable, all this plodding ranch culture deserves. Few Beethovens have emerged from the hill country, and those that don't stay on the farm become squeaky-clean, middle-class mechanics – doctors and bankers, mostly.

But lately there's an interesting white-trash element fraying the edges of the town, infecting the tidy nucleus of rock houses and immaculate lawns. Real mechanics are moving in. Where there's a dog, ticks will gather, smiles Lester as he savors his night with Mary Ann – an explosion of quiet blond water. It was strange having little Hugo in the next room. Lester thinks of little Hugo as a baby soldier with a paper hat and fife and fat legs marching bravely around the playroom to his mother's punctuated sighs and the slap of flesh on flesh.

Happy birthday to you, little boy, and she particularly sings when I roll her over.

What Lester needs is a software case strangely missing from Richard's 'effects.' Special effects, he smiles. A yellow Mustang convertible is parked on this same hill, two hundred yards away. The luck of the Irish. The cunning of the coyote. The dumbness of Deputy Welch, who told him Danny and Wendy were headed to Oatmeal. And now he's found the people who found what was left of Richard.

The couple on the hillside apparently think they're in a Clairol commercial. The girl is now turning in slow motion, and the man, or boy, stands too. A strange, warm wind lifts their hair as they move toward each other, and though he is too far away to tell for sure, Lester is confident that their eyes are as deep and serious as Lorne Green's selling Alpo, as Ricardo Montalban's in a Chrysler. He hops out of his Toyota, a pleasant fear creeping up his throat . . .

4

Hugo's due in Ozona at ten A.M. and has to hurry with his
Raisin Bran. Milk drips from Mary Ann's chin, and he
wonders why she prefers giving head lately, probably to be
done quickly. Anyway, he prefers this to the fake moaning.
What also bothers him is the afternoon aerobics class with
sexy TV girls casting a phosphorescent glow over the grinding field of cellulite that is her friends. It's weird. Mary Ann
looks beautiful – skinny even. But she works out real hard.
'Body Nazi,' he thinks. She's become a body Nazi, but
everybody needs a boost. And this is better than that bunch
who sat around looking up themselves with speculums,
talking about roses.

'Finish your orange juice, Hugo.'

Sometimes he's sorry he named the boy Hugo. He always
has to figure out which one she's talking to. And today
there's no telling; neither Hugo has finished.

Zooming out of Sonora, he flips on his fuzzbuster. You have
to entertain yourself or go mad. He plays 'Bust the Fuzz'
with Donny Durst, the cop in an arroyo one mile out of
town. It's an uncomplicated game, hard to lose. He thrills
equally at busting the fuzz and avoiding the radar, or
burning on through, unscathed, at ninety-five miles an hour.

*　*　*

A big metal pecan shimmers on the Ozona courthouse lawn. Across the street, Hugo drinks a Budweiser and orders catfish and greens in a dark back booth. It's nice to block out the West Texas sun, and Hugo tries to be hapy that he doesn't have a ranch like most of the kids he went to school with. From May to September it's just too hot to be fooling around with cattle, but then he remembers they're finding gas and oil on most ranches and he orders another beer. Right now Bobby Zesch and his wife are in France, pumping black gold out of their land long-distance, not a heifer in sight. He wonders if God actually thinks about who deserves to be born above a lake of oil. Probably not. God's probably too busy, and Hugo Daley will beat hot asphalt and come home to a joyless blowjob.

'You get a new dog, Hugo?' the waitress asks, nodding at a girl staring through the front window. The girl looks electrocuted, her hair a frozen explosion. 'Or has Mary Ann finally overdone it?'

Hugo has seen faces like this girl's on magazines at the checkout stand of the grocery store. He's seen them on TV. One or two around the school. Mascara sex. Ratty, smart-ass punks who like to look beaten up, like life was hard and they were crazy. Big deal.

'Dog,' he grunts.

On the road home, the image of the fly-splattered Jesus on the Mexican calendar lingers in his mind, and he is wondering what sort of things He truly did with Mary Magdalene when he sees the electrified girl again, hitchhiking with a big cat. He also sees she's chubby as well as startling, and he eases up on the gas in spite of the instant guilt he feels seeing girls hitchhike. He knows why he wants to stop.

She's sweating beyond the window, and she backs away

41

as the window rolls down, letting the cool air out into the desert.

'I'm headed to San Angelo!' he shouts as though into a storm.

'You a cop?' she asks, smacks gum.

'No.'

'Murderer?' She smacks again.

'Redneck. You wanna ride?'

'You wanna peeky-pooky?'

Hugo doesn't know if he wants to or not, but he has a few miles to think about it. Peeky-pooky? He might appreciate Mary Ann more, and there's a Trojan in the glove compartment.

'I like to clear the air right away. Nobody does nothing for nothing, and honesty's the best policy. My name is Chuckles. I travel a lot,' the girl says, scratching the cat. It appears to be a mix of Persian and Manx, splotched with oil. Sort of unrefined, Hugo thinks as he opens the cooler.

'Wanna beer,' he asks, popping one for himself. She nabs a Budweiser. Trying not to think, Hugo flips on the fuzzbuster and watches the desert jut by. Might as well be on a bus, he thinks, for all the talking.

'Ever blow a guy wearing a . . . you know?'

'You mean those flavored jobs?'

'Flavored jobs?' Hugo's never heard of them.

'Lemon. Apricot. Peach. Strawberry. Name it. Can I have another beer?'

Hugo looks hard at his passenger as he digs for beer. There's something about girls who drink beer and chew gum at the same time that isn't right. But it's a good idea about flavored rubbers. He regrets not having one now. Maybe he'd pay extra if she'd act happy. But he's embarrassed to seem provincial by asking her to do with a regular one. They smell funny. What if he broke down and let her do it without one?

42

Then what if he caught bugs and Mary Ann's teeth fell out, blink blink blink, just like that? He bets Bobby Zesch isn't having these problems in France. Rich guys could buy clean girls who combed their hair.

'You icing down your hand or what?'

Hugo jerks out of his trance in time to miss buzzards flapping off a dried rabbit.

'Sorry,' he says, pulling out a beer. 'Here you go.'

'You almost killed us.'

Chuckles seems dreamy, and when she smiles, she's actually pretty, in a child's way, like his girlfriend used to look after a football game – lost in a dream. But she's smiling because he almost killed her. He slows down.

'Scared?'

'Cops.'

Hugo first visualized his death as a tomato in his fifth year with the company, during a purge of the Yellow Pages salesmen, waiting for the 'ax to fall.' He was sort of hoping to be fired. But no, they called him 'a light in dark times.' He got a bonus that year and realized he would work for Southwestern Bell for the rest of his life. He lacked the courage to quit. No ax would fall. Nothing would happen suddenly in his life, not even his mother's and father's deaths, which seemed to be taking forever at the Horizon Home. There was no ax or bomb hanging over those poor souls. They were rotting like tomatoes, and it was just a matter of time before he rotted too. As he walked out of the nursing home one afternoon, he saw a big tomato in the sky and realized it was his tomato. The trick was to keep it fresh and shiny and on its invisible vine by keeping himself healthy. The tomato sort of hung over his head, trembling where the football used to be. He didn't always see it but he could feel it – an airy, crushing presence like God.

* * *

When little Hugo has to pee, he does the 'weenie dance.' Big Hugo feels like doing it himself and is glad the girl asks to stop. A girl who gets dreamy over death might pee on the seats. He pulls over, relieved as the cat flops out into the desert.

'Ever read any Casteneda,' she asks, squatting against the fender. 'About death over your left shoulder?'

'Nope.' Hugo scrambles down the bar ditch. In college he'd taken enough acid to make worms sing Handel, but he's not going to talk pop sorcery with a punk-brain. If they start in on this stuff, he might mention his tomato.

'Ever whisper to your pecker?' She leans across the hood with another beer, hip cocked. 'You got a pecker?'

'I wish I didn't,' he growls, tucking it in too soon. Unwanted droplets. There's almost a trickle down his thigh.

'Tuck it in too soon?'

'Screw you.' It just popped out. Hugo never said that to a girl before.

'Whatever for?'

Hugo's angry as he scrambles up the bank, trying to zip. 'Exactly. Let's go.'

'My cat.'

A corner of his shirttail is caught in the zipper. He fumbles behind the wheel.

'Forget it.'

'So leave.'

'Good luck,' Hugo snaps. He tosses her backpack through the door and sadly realizes the cooler is empty. But as he reaches over to slam the door the cat thumps into the front seat in an effluvium of dust and saliva.

'What luck,' she muses, sliding back in. 'Get in back, Herman.'

'It's gotta stay in back,' Hugo insists. 'It farts like a horse.'

'Mr Nice.'

'Sugar and Spice.'

'Screw,' she whispers.

'Whatever for?' He feels sort of bubbly as he squeals on to the asphalt, and the sun reddens like a tomato. Maybe little Hugo won't have a tomato. Maybe he'll be a joyful halfback. Tomato time. Tomato time. Heavenly shades of night are falling . . . It's tomato time. Out of the mist your voice is calling . . . tomato time . . .

'Can I turn on the radio?'

He's been singing.

'You've got a hit there. "Tomato Time." But please – '

'No disco, dammit,' he says, swinging into a 7–11. 'You pump, I'll pay. You're used to that.'

She grabs his arm as he stops. 'Let's stop bickering,' she says. 'It's boring.'

'Sure.' He opens the door but she grabs him, looks into his eyes.

'Beer,' she whispers. 'Ice.'

Beer, Hugo thinks. Ice. There is a lovely tongue behind this punkette's teeth. A tiny flicker. Hard. Soft. From a phone booth he rings his own phone on phone business. His wife tells him Lester called – he must go straight to Houston. Beer, he thinks, ice. He can see the phone by the bed. Mary Ann sleeps. In the phone booth he is scared. All the way to Houston? With this hooker? He imagines her wild hair as she works at belt level, unzipping him with her teeth. In San Francisco she probably went with girls even.

And all these truck stops!

'You look happier,' she quips as he slides behind the wheel.

'Well, I'm not. I've gotta make Houston by noon.'

'Lucky for me. Get anything to eat?'

'Wanna Snickers?'

Beer, he thinks, ice. The open road. The madcap Toad and

his canary yellow gypsy cart. Little Hugo loves the part of the *Wind in the Willows* when Toad gets run off the road by a carload of weasels. Instead of being mad, Toad is infatuated. 'Poop. Poop,' Toady mutters in happy delirium, mimicking the motorcar.

'Poop. Poop.'

'That the flip side of "Tomato Time"?' She pops a beer. '"Poop Poop"?'

'It's a story.'

'Your life?'

'Toad's.'

'Same deal.'

'Twat'

'Toad.'

'Beer.'

Chuckles opens a cold one, laughs at him.

Hugo's three hours out of Houston, and the girl and cat are sleeping. He pulls off at a Travel Lodge, little Hugo's favorite because of the bear in the nightcap. Hugo has trouble falling asleep in daylight and hurries through the registration, says the girl is his daughter, places a wake-up call for nine. The girl stumbles in, falls asleep in the other bed. Hugo sleeps. He dreams the Gulf of Mexico turns black as oil. Mary Ann wears little pontoon shoes as she skates across the surface in her aerobics gear. His own face is the sun half sunk or risen in the horizon – he can't tell which – but it is red, and children in pontoon shoes pepper him with raisins from their lunch sacks. Some throw whole boxes. His face reddens and swells. He's angry. Chains bind him to the ocean floor, and he stretches against them, slowly freeing himself from the muck. He is rising. Then, like the sun in cartoons, he pops above the black swell of ocean and smiles, turning the water gold and all the little sack lunches into gladiolas and lilies. It is too late to stop himself from coming. He wakes with his hands in wild hair and the phone ringing like his heaving heart.

'Nine o'clock, Mr Daley.'

In one hand he holds the phone, in the other the girl's still bobbing head.

'Thank you,' he puffs. Hangs up.

'You're welcome. One per four hundred miles. How's that? About one a day.'

He can feel himself suddenly free, driving around and around the world, hitting a Travel Lodge every eight hours for a blowjob. Sometimes a Hilton. How can he afford it? He sees them on boats, her in nice clothes. Some other girls. Life is gay. He is free at last. He floats above the slavery of the common world servicing telephone executives with good times. He's rich, and little Hugo's going to school in Switzerland.

Mary Ann crashes her Porsche.

'You need to cover for me for a couple of weeks, Hugo. Something's come up.' Hugo's feet sink deep in Lester's thick carpet. It's a nice office. Somehow life is improving. My Karma, he smiles. Nice deeds to weird hitchhikers pay off. Responsibility pays off. Love pays off. Hot dog. Oh, boy. Taxicabs!

'Good news, Chuckles. We're off to dine.' Hugo figures he'll call Mary Ann while Chuckles is in the shower.

'Dine?'

'Do you have a change of clothes?'

'Nothing proper.'

'Here. Take fifty. There's a mall across the street.'

She nabs the fifty and leaves so quickly that Hugo wonders if she's splitting for good, abandoning her farting cat.

He grabs the phone. 'Good news, Mary Ann.'

5

Good news puts it mildly. Thinking of Hugo gone for two weeks is closer to bliss than Mary Ann's been in a long time. To control her sudden elation she folds her long, blond hands in the lap of her nightie and thinks about the river of dreams – the river from which she emerged at about the age of eight, she thinks. It is a delicate place, and West Texas is hard on rivers. Wandering barefoot through what is now Georgia to California, Cabeza de Vaca, in 1532, called West Texas the most forbidding place made by God. Perhaps it had something to do with him being barefoot, but there are, for a fact, few rivers in West Texas – few wet ones anyway.

The river of dreams was her mind when she was a child, the mind of a natural dreamer. It was, she realizes, something special about her. She wants it back. She'd awakened from a daydream pregnant one morning when she was eighteen, after her first poke – a cowpoke. She married, pretending she loved somebody she didn't know, to make her folks feel better. After the divorce she felt obligated and guilty to both her parents and her child. The child died. She was lost, and there'd been something childlike about Hugo, even though he was sort of wild back then and talked about being free. She married him because he'd want a family and he seemed close to the river of dreams. As years passed, she discovered that his dreaminess was mainly stupidness, and by that time they had little Hugo . . .

* * *

'I wish I were a little more artsy. A lot of people don't think I'm very sensitive. Maybe little Hugo won't have a tomato.'

'Please be quiet,' whispers Chuckles.

'Sorry. I was thinking.' Maybe the little tyke will become a happy linebacker. 'I don't usually do this.'

'Should I tinkle on you?'

'No!' Hugo suddenly realized the vulnerability of his position. 'Do you tinkle on people a lot?'

'Some friends. More strangers.'

'You must have strange friends.' He shouldn't have let her on top. But no, he's a gentleman. She'd looked so little.

'They're okay. A little wet behind the ears.'

'That's kind of dirty, isn't it?'

Danny's hands smell like feet when he wakes up in the Liberty Bell Motel. It's a soft autumn day in Oatmeal. All his youth he wanted to stay in this motel, but there was no need. Motels meant voyages. People passed through in motels, bringing the atmosphere of distant places. A sense of the highway is in the shower, the instant coffee, the radio. He doesn't want to leave the room, doesn't want to be recognized, have folks ask what he's doing with his life. Why is it so difficult to lie to these people? Primordial guilt, that's why. This is where all his values got him. Most are still there. There's actually a heaven somewhere in the back of his mind, but it looks sort of like a bank.

'You were talking in your sleep, Danny.'

'I was dreaming about being awake.'

'"Wun, wabbit, wun!" you kept crying. "Wun! Wun! Wun!" Then you made little squealing noises, and sometimes you barked. "Woof! Woof! Woof!"'

'Ah. The rabbit dream. I haven't had the rabbit dream in years.'

'Must be a fierce rabbit. A black, killer rabbit.'

A pinwheel of blood.

'More than one. Four of them hold me down while the fifth thumps on my chest and sings "My Heroes Have Always Been Cowboys."'

'Evil rabbits.'

'Nasty rabbits.'

'Rabbits of doom.'

'My hands smell kind of like feet.'

'I had to put tennis shoes on your mitts to stop you from scratching your face in your sleep. Then you crawled around the room going "Woof! Woof! Woof!" I think coming home has made you edgy. You shouldn't drink so much. It inhibits your dreaming mechanism.'

'Dog therapy.'

'You locked yourself in this sweet old man's car and pressed your face against the back window and slavered. Most people would've called the cops.'

'Bastards.'

'I know, baby. I'm sorry. When you got out, you sniffed his tires. Licked his hand. And you cowered and whimpered when I came close – like you were abused as a puppy. You followed the old guy to his room, doing tricks.'

'Did I have friends?'

'Nope. The other dogs think you're phony. You and your shoes. They soaked the left rear tire good and gang-banged your doggy girlfriend, and she liked it. She's left you for good. Not even for money. You weren't enough. She likes biker dogs.'

Fido's grave is sunken, concave where it should be convex. The little cross is gone. Couldn't even bury him right, thinks Dan, remembering tossing sand at the big dog once, blinding it in one eye. The grave is under an oak tree on the back lot of Danny's old home, where it joins the far reaches of the

Edwards Plateau. Danny ponders digging up the grave, looking at the remains after all these years, as Emerson did his dead wife. Twice. Now that's optimism. Not in my case, he thinks. It's morbidness disguised as clarity. As though the morbidness cleansed me of the sadness of the truth: perhaps I have only loved quadrupeds.

Wendy is looking at him tenderly, then walks away when he notices, giving him privacy, such as it is. He is on a small hill above the town of Oatmeal, and this does not completely equate with privacy. A pickup is spinning up dust on the dirt road they just came up in the Mustang. People are about their business in the little town. Danny's uncle ran the grocery store so well, they made him president of the bank. He's dead now too. Like Big Sister and Poppy and Fido.

He found Poppy dead next to his overturned pickup, off a dirt road in the country, his neck broken, hugging the earth like an exhausted lover. Danny was passing through on his precious highway and stopped to say good-bye. He remembers Big Sister sitting and trembling – the hard, high, aristocratic nose and forehead and the suddenly childlike eyes above the immense familiar body that had cushioned him almost nightly as a boy. Trembling on the edge of the bed, she said, 'Now tell me again. I've got to get it clear. Poppy is dead. Poppy is dead. Poppy is dead . . .'

She looked so frightened and helpless that he found it hard to imagine that this was the woman he'd always felt had stifled his grandfather. Poppy had had a big love in him and deserved to love lots of people. He never got a chance to expand. There was a twinkle in his eye that a lot of the world could've used, Danny believed, but he'd grown diluted under Big Sister's anxious love. It hurt him to hurt her. So instead of playing, he'd drink. And he was often a schmaltzy drunk. Never mean but fairly inarticulate. And she didn't like that much either. But now she was alone, and Danny was sad for her like a child.

After the funeral he went on to Mexico where, every day at three, he mixed a drink and eased on to the terrace to study the paraplegic on the corner of Rio Tigris and Culiacan. Mexico City was hot, and beneath the umbrella, wired to the back of his motorized wheelchair, the cripple clutched a cocktail. But in the ten days before Danny spoke to him, he never once took a sip. To Danny he seemed somehow symbolic, frozen in his wheelchair – a metaphor for trapped love.

Through the bougainvillea that lined his terrace wall, Danny could see moisture bead the cripple's glass, and when he had a spasm, if the traffic was hushed, he could hear the rattle of ice cubes. At first he wondered what the poor guy was doing out there, when everyone else had drifted into cool, dark rooms, but he was afraid to ask. The man's upper lip was a snarl, and one eye rolled sightlessly as he appeared to listen for something behind the walls. On several occasions Dan was certain the guy heard him get up to mix another gin and tonic. One day it just popped out: 'What are you doing?'

This really rattled his cubes. His neck wrenched around, but when he couldn't see Danny, he clawed a lever, spun the chair around and puttered up to the wall. His good eye searched the leaves.

'I hope I didn't frighten you.' Danny gulped.

Nothing.

'I'm from the United States. Don't have anyone to talk to. I'm sorry if I was rude.' His eye found Danny's face, and something happened in his lower lip that might have been a smile.

'Is that drink just for show? What are you doing out here at siesta?' By moving his head slightly, Dan could make the leaves blot out the twisted face. Christ, he thought, his mind is probably jelly.

'I'm sorry. I didn't know you couldn't speak. I don't even know if you can understand me. Do you ever drink out of that glass?'

He strained to lift his drink, ice cubes clattering like castanets, and while he struggled, Dan took a drink of his own. The cripple spilled liquid over his chin and chest but eventually got a good swallow.

'Cheers,' said Dan.

He seemed to smile again, and Dan felt relieved but was running out of talk.

'If you'd like some company, I have a suggestion. I'm working on a story, and it helps me to read aloud. You might like it – it's about a man who thought his body caused trouble. His wife institutionalized him after driving him crazy in an open marriage. The sexual variety was pleasant, but the intimacies that grew out of the sex, which made him feel like his heart was growing, threatened her, and knowing him as well as she did, she could tell when he fell in love, which he did. Cold, gymnastic sex was fine. It was the love that angered her. She was losing her handle. She got him so crazy that now he fears anything both sexual and loving and actually prefers the straitjacket. Whenever his memories become unbearable, he imagines that someone splits his skull with a shovel, spades him into a garden of cabbages. He loves decay. Let me read you a passage.'

Dan made a drink on the way in to get the manuscript. When he got back to the terrace, the cripple was still there. He read: 'Anna sits before me, her hair done up as it was five years ago. Even after having me committed, she needs me, the detached observer. She says Angela, our lover, was out to replace her, that she felt she was drowning. This makes cabbages creep close, but though I crave death, I

53

ignore the vegetables long enough to give her that dose of honesty she seeks. "You're a bitch," I say. This humiliates and, in some strange way, purges her. She perks up enough to stare out my hospital window and look tragic. Leaves are beginning to fall, and men hustle beneath the far trees with rakes and baskets. Soon Anna will turn her gaze from the mournful autumn and say that perhaps I'm right, perhaps everybody competes.'

Through the leaves, the cripple's eye glistened, and young Danny felt he'd done okay. He apologized again for startling him and said he hoped he liked the irony in the bit about the straitjacket. Then he offered to read again the next day, said good-bye and closed the door to the terrace.

The shades on the windows tinted the room a murky green. Coming in from the terrace, Danny normally experienced the feeling that he was under water. This was nice. When he sat down to type, the green light eased the flow and he could feel the lurking monsters of his imagination. But after talking to the paraplegic, the air seemed dry and thin. Something had changed. He fixed himself another drink and waited. Nothing happened. Like the night of his grandfather's death, he got cold and hollow. He edged back to the window. The cripple was gone. Danny needed to get out. In the street, amputees scooted about like spiders. There were dirty, hungry children everywhere. A couple of policemen kicked a shoeshine boy, and Dan headed to the mountains, thinking maybe the cripple had it easy. Fewer decisions – maybe it's a form of freedom.

Dusk rose from the gutters and the day softened as he came to the fields at the base of the hills and waded through good, burning dirt. Feeling he could breathe again, he stopped at the edge of a ditch, lined by tall eucalyptus trees, deeply matted by rotting eucalyptus leaves. It was too wide to jump across, so he hopped down but sank to his neck in an open sewer. The strong smell of rotting eucalyptus leaves eclipsed, for a moment, the odor of Mexico City's most essential filth, and it took him a while to figure out just how disgusting it was. Then he slogged up the opposite bank, but there he was, ten miles from his apartment, in the middle of nowhere, covered with shit. For the first time since Poppy's death he felt like crying. He sat down.

Dogs ran out from some shacks across the fields, and children followed but turned back when they smelled him. When he reached the houses, an old man leveled a pistol at him.

'*Necessito agua*,' Danny cried.

The old man nodded but kept the piece leveled.

'I fell into the ditch. I am covered with shit.'

People filtered between the shacks, but at the end of a choked alleyway Danny could see a water pump in the plaza. He put his hands up, and they backed away as he walked through, crying. He could feel Poppy decomposing in the ground.

Beneath the pump in the deepening mud, he convulsed in the water, still startled beyond reason. Then they began to stone him. The evening turned white as he thrashed through a thicket of cactus up the mountain behind the village and the sun set over Mexico City. Halfway up the slope, as he pulled himself over a ledge, he bumped into a dog that had been hung by the neck from an ugly tree, its eyes deep masses of swarming flies. It wasn't Fido. On top of the mountain was a big cross. Scattered beneath it were news-papers, beer cans, rubbers. To the east a path wound down the slope, but he found a fatal cliff to the west. He was going to end it. A cool updraft pressed his face as he sat down, hung his legs over the edge.

The bus ride back to the city was embarrassing.

He drank for several days, maybe longer, after he came

down off the mountain. Late one night, when he'd passed out in the cantina, the woman who sang there woke him up and took him home with her. They slept beneath a statue of the Madonna. The singer was older, and when he talked about wanting a larger life, she told him that he was looking for something adolescent.

'You say we are trapped,' she said. 'Ha. You want girls to think they are trapped by the flesh so they will rebel against it, as you specify. And not by abstaining.'

He knew she turned tricks for the owners of the bar, or at least entertained their gangster friends, but she was not like the other whores who came and went with a man every thirty minutes. In the bar he could tell she felt superior to the other girls by the way she paid for his drinks. In front of everyone she called him her 'Cordobes,' after the bullfighter.

Though he couldn't talk to her about the trap or how to escape it, sometimes at night, when he lay awake and she was sleeping, when he got that frozen feeling thinking about his grandfather, he made it go away by pulling her close, and when he entered the autumn of her body, he thought of all the other men she'd had, of their women, their children.

But sometimes, when all he could see was the cripple, frozen in the wheelchair with his drink, he'd pretend that he himself was his grandfather and that the woman beneath him, with her high, aristocratic forehead, was his grandmother.

Fido's ghost lumbers in the warm wind, as transparent as hummingbird semen. The old dog never had moved too fast. Like Poppy. It's hard. You can't love everybody. And it's full-time work to love just one.

Meanwhile, away from the grave, Wendy is chanting quietly. Is she, Danny wonders, jealous of Fido?

* * *

Out of gas? Danny thinks. An unpleasant experience. Both thinking and being out of gas. One for me, one for him. Who is this, he wonders, looking at Lester. Nick Nolte with a blow dryer?

'Is that right?' he says. 'No gas? That's a bitch.' Wendy's left breast nuzzles backward. Her eyes zero back. This guy interrupted a tender moment by Fido's sad grave.

As they drive Lester to town for gas, Les fumbles with a newspaper, looks out the window, then asks, 'What brings you this way?'

'The highway.'

'And the Mustang,' Les laughs. 'Why, really?'

'I got drunk. Curious.'

'It's sort of sick to be curious about Oatmeal.'

'I'm sick.'

'Me too. A buddy of mine was just murdered up by Menard. It's right here on the front page. Pretty ugly.'

Wendy grabs the paper. 'That's the guy we found. What was left of him.'

'Found? You guys found him?' Lester looks incredulous. 'You poor kids.' Wendy reads the article. Danny taps the steering wheel.

'He was a good guy,' muses Lester.

'Too bad.'

'He had a sense of humor.'

'I'm sorry.'

'My friend.'

'Hey. Sing a sad song about it.'

'Who pulled your string?'

'You did. I don't wanna talk about it.'

'I can understand that.'

'You'll have to excuse Danny,' pleads Wendy. 'That was his dog's grave back there.'

6

Chuckles drifts through Penney's picturing a twenty-five-dollar Lauren Bacall outfit. It's what this dancing bear Hugo wants. Ah, the road. The highway of life. She's surprised Hugo didn't shout at her to pick up some rubbers as she crossed the parking lot.

In the dressing room she tries a green shift that makes her taller. She pulls her hair back like a lady lawyer. Bit of lace. Poor Hugo. Down you go, round and round you go. A child peeks through the dressing room drapes, and Chuckles realizes she's singing in front of the mirror. This is sick, she thinks, remembering David's mirrors, the big blacks. The small blondes. Suck on that, sucker. She can picture David bouncing around his house smashing lamps, a frantic hollowness blossoming inside him. He can't kill it with cocaine, she knows. She got him. She got him good.

David is snorting lots of cocaine, bouncing around his house in San Francisco, smashing lamps. Chuckles got him good. Not only can't he kill the memory of her with coke, he can't kill it with little girls, big girls, middle-sized girls, or any permutation or combination thereof, even with big black guys. It all seems very unfair.

Why be awake in all this unfairness? he reasons. Heroin. Oh boy, oh boy. Now I'm a real person with real problems. I've got emotion. Nobody can say I'm superficial no more. I be soul American. I be riding in my Lincoln. Baby Chili be driving. Crisco be chopping. I be grieving behind my shades. We be looking fo' jive. We be looking to off de pain. My man's pain.

I'd give my left nut to be a nigger, thinks David as they swing into a big circle drive in Oakland. My left nut. He can still see Chuckles flirting in front of the camera. There was a girl who liked her work. Liked it too much, really. Sure he directed the films, but she did little things with her eyes that took it out further. People fell in love with her. He couldn't direct that. She made movies within movies. That's why she was so good. A perfect chameleon. Even dykes went all goo-goo. She liked to get them the best. The hard types. She melted 'em. Opened 'em up. Brought out the longing child, the mother. He'd come in his pants several times, just watching her work. Once he knew she was with some other guys without him, clear across town; and in the middle of his drive to go get her, in the middle of his ache and anger on the freeway, he imagined what she was doing, and he came without an erection.

He was crying.

Chuckles flounces into the bathroom to get sophisticated. Hugo is all dressed up, watching *Gunsmoke*. He's excited and seems to have toned down the shaving lotion.

'Ready to go, Ralph?'

He likes her dress, she realizes.

'I like your dress.'

'That all?'

He takes her to the Sheraton and leaves champagne on ice at the Travel Lodge, though it's less than romantic when he reveals the truth about the bear in the nightcap.

'The beer and the nightcap,' she asks. 'Your little boy drinks?'

'No, no. You misunderstood.'

She winks. He blushes.

'I tease a lot. The truth hurts.'

Confusion on his big face. If he was any swifter, she thinks, he could tie his shoes.

Pokey. Pokey. Pokey. The big ying yang won't go away. She actually came herself, she muses. When you get over the shock of what a goof he is, close your eyes a little, Hugo's a pleasant enough big guy. He's cuddly. It's odd. Who does he think I am? she wonders. The Bear in the Nightcap? Hugo needs a teddy bear. He'll be a mess tomorrow. He got carried away and forgot to use rubbers, and now he's probably dreaming about AIDS – his wife's hair falling out and his own eyeballs sinking back into the cavernous skull and past his shrinking brain and dropping out a wizened rectum, bouncing like strange marbles on the floor. And what about 'Tomato Time'? Heavenly shades? She curls next to him. Odd. Very odd to be cuddled.

From the backseat of the Lincoln, David looks up the long walkway from the top of the big circular drive and feels helpless. The last two weeks of coked out, heartbreaking partying have left him weak and frazzled. The orgies just felt meaty without her, until he'd done tons of drugs. Then he often couldn't feel anything. He wishes he were lying beside Chuckles in his bed. He liked the way she looked when she slept. She crashed so completely. Sprawled against the mattress, she looked like a drowned butterfly – something frozen in mid-motion. Often he would lie awake in the morning and just look at her and laugh. Even with her eyes closed she had the intensity of a hard-playing child, and he couldn't imagine what she was dreaming. It was funny and frightening. Her dreams must be weirder than her waking imagination, he figured, and that must really be wild. He would study her in awe and watch the movements of her eyes beneath her lids in incredible curiosity.

The pretty Filipino girl, Baby Chili, sits behind the wheel looking at her nails and humming to herself. She's glad Chuckles is gone. David knows. And so is Crisco, the big, beautiful mulatto den mother of his operation, who is sitting beside him chopping up lines on the foot-long fold-out mirror in the back of the Lincoln.

He looks again up the long walkway beneath gauzy mimosas, through rows of brilliant acacias, and doesn't feel like walking all that way, even for heroin. Why couldn't they stash a little golf cart down at the driveway for guests? A blue one, say, with a red canopy. Two steps out of the Lincoln he stops, turns back to the car.

'Give me one more big one, Crisco.' He ducks his head in the back window, hoovers up, then feels like he can make it.

Olander O. answers the big double doors himself and gives David a big hug, replete with slaps on the back. David can smell Olander's cologne, or whatever the hell it is, and it doesn't go well with his hangover. A spoiled little Venezuelan from a rich family, he has tripled his family's considerable wealth, without ever jeopardizing it, in the smack trade. Olander gives new dimension to the word *oily*. He likes David because of the movies, the girls.

'*Ola. Que tal, amigo?* You look beat.'

'Chuckles left.'

'Drop in the bucket. Come in. You want a drink?'

'I want some junk.'

'You don't want no junk.'

David looks at him.

'You're right. You want some junk.'

* * *

61

Herman looks so relaxed, thinks Chuckles. It took a while to talk Hugo out of the Travel Lodge, but this La Quinta is nicer, and not that much more expensive. Plus, they just charge her calls to the room, no questions asked. That's her, Mrs Hugo. Calling San Francisco to torment naughty David and calling room service. She's finally getting caught up on her soaps: Theresa, that's the girl on *Nights of Darkness*, had been kidnapped by her ex-husband's stepmother and ransomed to her husband for $724,000, but immediately after her release she got run over by her aunt, who was backing out of the driveway on the way to a movie. Now Theresa is paralyzed and her husband is falling in love with her ex-husband, who owns a Dodge dealership, and the stepmother is coughing up $51,405 toward the medical bills. None of the bitches' makeup was badly damaged, and the tragedy is bringing everyone closer together. Just as Hugo and Chuckles are growing closer, she muses. He's enlightening her about football.

She'd heard there were bimbos in Texas. And some bad guys. And some bad bimbos. But Hugo makes her wonder what the girls are like. Not her kind of girls, you know. But the tight little housewives in the trailers and such. Hugo's wife tickles his noogies on Christmas and won't work or go fishing. Obviously she tickles a mean noogie.

It's a smooth-riding automobile, and Crisco shoots up David neatly, says 'Mmm' as she watches the heroin warmth come over him, and Baby Chili heads the Lincoln in the general direction of Texas, which she's heard is more or less south. David had Chuckles's calls traced. He's got more connection than a snake. Right now he's nodded out in the backseat, his head in Crisco's lap. He needed that heroin. So did she and lovely Crisco. To shut him up a goddamn minute.

Chili's nervous about Texas. Keeps the speed down. You hear so many different things. What's a girl to believe? David isn't exactly protected down there, she suspects, and everybody carries guns and shoots Mexicans. Being Filipino, she's concerned. Damn that Chuckles.

Yesterday Hugo brought some videos home from the office. Now he's trying to improve her, she realizes. Some junk on the value of a college education, another about saving for the future, another about hard work. Nearly as exciting as driver training films, but she got kinda wet, and before you know it, she and Hugo were at it again, making like panthers in heat. He used to be embarrassed in front of mirrors, but he pulled the dresser mirror down and set it against the headboard and even tied her up a little with a couple of his belts. There she was with this monster dick in her little mouth and Hugo working away on her tiny thingie and a Billy Graham type pounding a pulpit in the video in the mirror and shouting about savings accounts.

During the college education flick she put her hair up in pigtails and wore this little white pinafore and did her Little Bo Peep routine without undies, and Hugo went ape. He was big. Nobody had ever played with his imagination before. It was fun.

When she and David used to make films with these big guys and sometimes other girls, it was kind of neat to see herself lusted on. They'd hold her in different ways, and instead of feeling used, like it was sometimes meant to seem, she felt a kind of power. They needed her. And David thought he had the power by having her. She knows that. And some of the films were good, others just boring. The good ones had tension, something happening in the eyes of the people. She could do their emotions. That was the good part, she knows, breaking through something. But what are you breaking through with savings account lectures?

7

Somehow the world is bigger. Hugo's younger. He stares at
Chuckles sleeping beside him. She's elflike. He laughs, filled
by a pleasant chaos. A lot of his life disappeared, but he
doesn't feel older. He feels like a large, tricked child. He can
see Skipper, his childhood buddy, taunting him from the
limbs of a great fallen tree where they used to play Cowboys
and Indians or War, depending on the movie they'd seen
that weekend. Skipper laughs from the tree: 'Betcha don't
know where I hid that last twenty-five years, do you, Hugo?'

The tree lay by a small, dry creek just beyond the outskirts
of town. Even on its side, the branches that rose from the big
cypress were higher than the surrounding oaks. Hollowed
out beneath the trunk was Skipper and Hugo's hideout, a
cool place on long summer afternoons. A place away from
the town, the houses.

Hugo was fascinated by the border between the town and
the country and used to try to feel the difference when he
passed from one into the other — as though there were a
force field or something. When he moved from the blistered
hillside down through the cactus and came within sight of
the courthouse dome and entered the back lot of Votter's
machine shop, with its smell of grease and metal and its
mysterious sounds, he grew nervous. The awesome vastness
of the great, still countryside gave way to something distract-
ing, but he couldn't explain it. They were smarter than he

was, these people who ran the town and churches and banks. And though he didn't understand it, he felt that his life would always depend on odd forces.

The grease and metal and grinding gears in Votter's shop somehow represented the town and how it worked. Something he couldn't comprehend. Like a complex metal monster eating the trees, covering the ground with asphalt and concrete excretions. He sometimes wondered if the point was to turn the world into a concrete marble. Maybe God didn't like earth. Maybe that's why you got all stiff and starchy for church.

Suddenly he laughs. Chuckles looks like an imp and makes him feel like a kid. It's a great big world, happy and loose. Skipper's laughing. Everybody has dirt on their knees and their cheeks are smudged and they're laughing. But that strange smell of the machine shop comes back to Hugo, and for the first time it reminds him of the smell of the melting Teflon-coated Grease Filters, which in turn reminds him of the days of the blood business and the odor of burning guinea pigs. He grows solemn and reflective. The odor of burning guinea pigs is distasteful, of course, but it's also a door to his childhood. His father and uncle got into the blood business to supplement the meager income from their tiny farm. You got thirty-seven fifty a liter for sheep's blood, fifty dollars a gallon for horse, fifty cents a cc for guinea pig. They also bled rats, chickens and the occasional rabbit.

Sheep's blood is similar to human blood, and for this reason laboratories use it to make the culture into which the doctor drops the cotton swab after he has swabbed the back of your throat to check for strep infection. You bleed the sheep by shaving a patch of wool off its jugular vein. Your helper clamps the beast between his knees and grabs its ears and twists its head so the vein pops out. You stick it with a needle attached to a tube that leads to a vacuum-sealed sterile gallon jar. You can bleed a quart of blood out of a normal sheep before it gets woozy. Then you're supposed to mark it so you won't bleed it for a week. But sheep only cost fifteen dollars apiece, and it was hard to bleed them on cold nights, which was when Hugo and his cousins had to bleed, since the daylight was occupied working elsewhere. If a sheep refused to hold still, Hugo's cousin would sometimes bleed it till it dropped.

They bled the smaller animals in the basement of his uncle's big house, since it had a furnace. Hugo and his parents lived in a cabin. It was warm in the basement of his uncle's house, but Hugo didn't like bleeding the guinea pigs because their veins were so small. You had to stick the big needle right into their hearts, and a lot of them croaked on the spot. These they tossed into the furnace, producing a brief but memorable odor, rather like the odor that filled the kitchen of the Downtowner Motor Inn the day Hugo lost his first million. Since he lost the million dollars before he ever really had it, and since he never made a second or third million to lose either, it's a fairly important memory. He remembers it clearly.

Alex, the manager of the restaurant, pointed to a green glob of metal mesh that dropped from the bank of grease filters above the broilers. After three months the intense heat of the broiler had melted the Teflon-coated Grease Filter Hugo invented, the filter that would change his life by making him rich, the most ecological grease filter in the evolution of grease filters. And the easiest to clean. The other filters seemed to be in the early stages of a similar decomposition. The whole bank looked cancerous.

'I want my money back,' said Alex.

Alex seemed pretty mad, and since it was the second time he'd mentioned wanting his money back, Hugo figured that some of the camaraderie he'd developed with Alex over the last three months had vanished. This was disturbing. He'd stopped in to check on the filters and have a coffee every week and had thought he'd befriended Alex. On top of that, Corky, Hugo's salesman, sold these same filters to every restaurant in Amarillo, Lubbock and Abilene. Corky was, at that moment, in Chicago, at the National Restaurant Convention, selling the same filters to nationwide chains like Denny's, McDonald's, and JoJo's. All of the new company's profits had been used to salary him and send him there. For Grease Filters Inc. to refund the money for all the filters would be a difficult, if not impossible, task.

'I want my money back.' That was three times.

'Alex, you'll get your money back. This isn't too good for me either, you know.'

On his way home to tell Mary Ann they weren't going to be rich, Hugo tried to summon up a little of the old cowboy spirit he hoped was left over from his youth in the country. He used to wake up an hour and a half before dawn to help his dad with the chores. In the early-morning darkness he always felt a little special. Even when the farm failed and he moved to San Angelo to drive a bakery route, he felt a little like a cowboy when he woke up early and drove through the dark suburbs alone. In the bakery truck he listened to Merle and Willie, and even after being away from the farm for twenty-five years, he kept talking like a cowboy. Though he made good money on the route and was once named Salesman of the Month, he thought a real man should have his own business. It was the American spirit.

So he started a candy-apple factory. He sold candy apples to shops along his bakery route and at football games, and he liked the machine that made the candy apples, a machine he helped design. It looked like a chrome octopus and spun around like a carnival ride. In each arm it held a pointed stick, and to run it all you needed was one Mexican, who sat by a box of fresh apples and stuck them on as the pointed sticks whirled past. Once the apples were stuck, the arms spun them around on their axes like little planets, and the octopus whirred around in circles, passing the spinning apples through vats of red goo and crushed nuts.

He made a nice side living off the apples and joined a country club where he met other double-knit businessmen and went in on some other deals with them. He liked that. Mary Ann liked it. She liked to dress up and go to the club. He knew folks thought he was a redneck, but he was trying to get them to think he was a 'crafty old country boy.' He knew they thought he worked hard and was ambitious. Hadn't he moved up from the bakery route to selling Yellow Pages for Southwestern Bell? And his candy-apple business showed industry, even if it was a little common. Making millions of dollars on newly invented grease filters would've proved he was smart once and for all.

But he felt stupid. The Teflon-coated Grease Filter over Alex's broiler looked like the belly of a dead frog he'd once thrown at his little brother. One night he'd been gigging frogs in the cattle tank by the windmill when his little brother sneaked up and scared him. He spun around so quickly that the frog he'd speared flew off the gig and sailed past his brother's head into the willows, where they found it the next morning, dripping through the branches, bloated and covered with flies, looking just like a melting Teflon-coated Grease Filter. And it smelled bad. It smelled like burning guinea pigs. It smelled like Votter's machine shop. These memories sadden Hugo. And it seems there is a bad smell in the motel room too. Hugo turns from Chuckles to spy Herman the ugly cat lumbering out from under the bed. Damn, he thinks. Darn that cat.

* * *

Hugo opens the windows to the motel room and sneakily locks the farting cat in the bathroom. Then he turns on the air conditioner full blast. It smells almost worse than burning guinea pigs, but soon the air clears and his spirits elevate. He feels like laughing again as he looks at Chuckles. She's quite something. And she likes him, he thinks. She actually likes him a little.

It's these unexpected, unplanned things that keep you young. Off-guard. Loose. He's reminded of a feeling he'd had on the verge of being rich, when he thought the Teflon-coated Grease Filters were going to secure his life forever. He was having lunch at the club a week after he'd donated a set of filters to the club's kitchen, and the maître d' had come to the table and congratulated him on his fine invention – for they hadn't yet begun to melt. He was dining with associates, and everybody got up to go into the kitchen and look at the clean green banks of filters above the grill and broiler. The long years of cold mornings along the bakery route, the arched eyebrows when he'd confided that he made candy apples and the struggle of his own marriage suddenly seemed an integral part of his success.

'I'm glad they're working out for you,' said Hugo humbly. 'Now when we gonna go fishing?'

Back at the plush table, he'd experienced a dizzy elation looking out the huge window on to the golf course. But then, suddenly, he felt like he had after he'd broken a horse for his dad, when the old man could no longer ride. It was merely a matter of getting back on, every time he'd been thrown, and taking his chances. A curious love and hate had bound him to the thrashing, twisting stallion. Once he'd broken it, however, once it submitted, loping across the land in the evening light, responsive to his rein, Hugo experienced a sadness that was hard to describe.

Something wild had gone out of his life.

8

Lester has slipped into his awareness trance, put on his easygoing façade, put his mouth on automatic pilot for harmless chatter and he's into an almost dreamlike state in which all his inner senses are primed to the atmosphere and people around him. Wendy and Danny seem perfectly harmless. Children, he thinks. Lucky me. It isn't easy for Lester to relax. Unless he's under the gun, he wonders what to do with himself. How much simpler to cut their throats, rifle their bags, get the software case and be done with it. But then again, he's not really sure they have the software with Richard's secret, or even the case. It's just a chance. Still, it would be quicker to cut their throats and get on with the search. But no. They've been seen together, now that they're driving through Oatmeal toward the gas station. That's a problem. And Lester's not really into throat cutting unless it's a matter of convenience.

In one of his experiments with the videos, Richard had drummed up a snuff-flick gang out of Colombia and, unbeknownst to Les, had a real live snuff tracked beneath a section of a Bill Cosby show. Just as old Bill was giving his kid a lecture on honesty, Lester began to puke. Richard showed it to him later – a pale boy impaled on a giant pederast while a couple more effeminate types toyed with him until he helplessly ejaculated. Just as the boy came, they cut his throat.

The boy had looked so simply sad and so simply dead that when Les quit puking, he told Richard the video was in bad taste and that something like that might make a sicko actually do something violent. But Les was working on detachment and forced himself to watch it over and over again until he could keep from throwing up. So he isn't really into throat cutting, he realizes, and tries to take it easy. He tries to seem melancholy and euphoric, waiting for his chance to get the case without hurting Wendy and Danny. The girl is nice-looking.

Relax, he tells himself. Take it easy. 'Beautiful day,' he says.

Danny can see himself as a child by the ancient coke machine at the filling station. This Arco used to be a Mobilgas, and there used to be a big green concrete star full of water and goldfish at the edge of the oily apron on the corner of Rainy Street and Highway 87. Big Sister wouldn't let him cross the highway, so he'd go beneath it through a great spider-filled culvert that was cool even in the heat of day.

Sometimes he'd sit under the highway for a while, with a stick nearby to splat the spiders, and listen to the immense wheels blasting overhead. He could feel the tremors of wheels all the way to San Antonio, and if he closed his eyes, the colors and shapes of the continents spun through the dark. Chinese reached through the cool ground, Arabs flew winged horses and he knew he didn't have enough lives, that he was trapped. But maybe, he hoped, the highway overhead also ran through his head like roots and the trails of jets.

A tattered pile of *National Geographic*, pilfered from Big Sister's collection, lay on a ledge above the water level, just in case it ever rained. Fido loved it there, and Danny would

sit with one hand on the happy old dog and turn the pages
with the other . . .

'Regular or unleaded?'

He has gone into something of a trance by the gasoline
pumps. The new, shiny pumps. Not the rusted cylindrical
pumps with the glass cylinder filling before your very eyes,
with the winged Mobilgas horse flying off the top as you
stood on the baking concrete and watched Uncle Egan's
body warp in fumes as he pumped startlingly clear fluid into
a brand-new Oldsmobile with South Dakota plates . . .

'Regular or unleaded?'

'Sorry. Regular.' It's a '65 Mustang.

'And a case of Budweiser,' chimes Lester. 'And five
gallons of unleaded to go. And a bag of ice. I'm buying.'

His chief dread is bumping into an old acquaintance and
having to make conversation. What would he say? What
have you been doing here all these years? What would they
say? Too good for us, Danny? The older folks, what was left
of his grandparents' friends, would be easier. You could still
swap clichés and be comfortable. There's some grace in that.

'No great loss,' Wendy says.

'Huh?' Danny looks around him.

'Lester said you'd lost your concentration.'

'No hurry,' says Lester, 'but I don't think they'll let us park
here to drink. This Bud's for you.'

Danny puts it in gear. Drinking is nice, and drinking with
a new person. Even though Lester somehow disgusts him.
Mustn't be close-minded, though. If you avoided everything
that bothered you, you'd turn into soggy toast or oatmeal.

'Where do you want to drink?'

They drink by the river, where everybody's pretty quiet.
Danny watches Lester work at being wistful. The twilight
helps, and it is good that Lester doesn't talk. He seems to be
trying to establish a sense of intimacy as he hunkers against

a mesquite, brooding into the sunset, rolling little pebbles around in his fist and tossing one, every once in a while, into the river.

Wendy has seen Danny getting dreamy. A sort of possum routine he goes in around people he doesn't like. Guarded types. He draws them out with somnolent goofiness, then mocks them.

'Danny, let's go. It's getting dark.'

'Lester wants to commune.'

'Cow pucky.'

'Are you sad, Lester?'

She can see anger in Lester's eyes. But it's quickly gone, and it's not imagination. Lester works on some permanent cold rage he probably doesn't even know exists.

'Beyond sad.'

'Myself, I'm so smart and sensitive that I'm deeply sad always. You can tell by looking into my eyes. And look at my eyelids. Poetic.'

'Exquisite lids, Danny.' Lester takes a swig and looks away from Danny into the sky. His body seems to loosen. He's back in control. 'Why are you picking on me?' He flicks a pebble into the river. 'I'm nice.'

Danny is sitting on the hood of the Mustang, leaning against the windshield, star peeping.

'Fido's dying quiver.'

This could be a problem, thinks Wendy as Danny breaks out a Budweiser. He starting to get curious.

'What do you do?'

'I work.'

'Can't be too careful.'

Jesus, Wendy thinks, why can't Danny lay off? She moves through the night toward the river where a full moon seems to rock in the channels. When she was a little girl, she waded the rivers of the San Joaquin with her father at night and thought of the dark waters around her ankles stroking down into an ocean that splashed laughing Micronesians and pressed Australia and India beneath stars like brilliant oranges.

Lester studies the age in Danny's eyes, what there is of it, as he weaves countercultural prattle. Trying to draw this one out isn't easy. Danny has perfected a childishness that insulates him nicely. He seems a lot more spontaneous than he actually is, Lester calculates, but who knows? Maybe his façade has annealed itself to his soul. This happens. Maybe he's become a kid. How nice for him. Maybe he can enter into the kingdom of heaven along with the rest of the grapefruits of bliss.

It could be worse, he figures. Danny could think he was intellectual or mystic. Instead he pretends to have given up. It makes him hard to handle. He has too much fun. Fuck him, thinks Lester.

What's Wendy up to? She babies him, that's what. She wants an intelligent, quasi-mystical baby who doesn't kick ass, a nice, sensitive guy. Some adventurers, Lester thinks, and shuts up. Looks at the stars. Looks at Wendy.

Her shirt is wet from the river, and her breasts are lovely and so are her nipples. But she's too wholesome. You need a little sleaze, by golly, a little self-conscious sexuality, however shallow, just to communicate these days. People don't understand you otherwise. It's like talking without a vocabulary. We can thank Joan Collins and such for that. If you don't come off like a super-slick nut-cutter, you don't come off at all. What a life. But, he must admit, Joan Collins beats the hell out of the Ann Arbor faculty wives – a collection of Joni Mitchells gone to seed. A Methodist swap club. A gaggle of poetic geese. Just once he'd wanted to see a little passion or humor in that vapid, prune-faced sincerity, just a sparkle.

Two years after he got back from Vietnam, shortly after he dropped first the heroin and then the aristocracy scam, Lester became a cop in the El Paso Sheriff's Department because his parents wanted him to go to graduate school. Doctors of psychology at the University of Michigan, his mother and father were all charts and graphs and chatter. Knee-jerk liberals, they preferred their emotion in print. So Lester became a cop in the lovely, gritty town right next to some startling cruelty and poverty in Juarez, to get close to the real world.

In the crime-search unit he was required to make photographs of the corpses, the bloated and beaten and decomposed. So in the interest of psychology he sent copies of the photos to his parents of raped children, mass murders, kinky corpses. It was nasty, but you either looked or lived a lie. This was an exercise in making himself both aware and hard.

His favorite photo was the Dempsey Dumpster flambé. The victim had been soaked in gasoline, locked in the dumpster, set afire and had survived. He looked like a jellyfish in the plastic, water-filled sack in which he was suspended in the hospital. And that was *after. Before* was better. Four hard cops blew lunch when they opened the lid on this guy.

These and other pictures that chronicled his three years in the El Paso Sheriff's Department were tucked away in a box in his parents' basement. He sometimes felt guilty about sending them because as he'd grown older, he'd started to forgive his folks for sheltering him, and he knew he did it to shock. But his mother never asked him *not* to send them. Both his parents pretended to be interested in the cases, and when he visited, they'd have coffee over the photographs.

Before his arrival, they'd bring the box of pictures up from the basement, especially for his visit, and place it in his father's study, as though his father kept it there. He knew the pictures made them squeamish, and it gave him satisfaction when he thought of the box of photos symbolically, as existing in many such basements, in many such houses, owned by many of the same kinds of people – the kind who looked haunted and soulful after poetry readings about poverty and carnage. You didn't need a poem about poverty in Juarez.

Wendy drifts to the river where Danny ran trotlines with his grandfather at night, and Danny thinks how the old man and the darkness and the river somehow bend back in time until the memories and the stories about him intertwine until you can't tell the difference, and new dreamlike visions replace the old like the curling currents of the river, and the power of the river is constant through the rocks, white in the moonlight. This, too, is a kind of fishing.

Poppy would take him in the late afternoon to Comanche Creek, to seine for bait, and they'd be drinking cold cans of Budweiser from an oil drum full of block ice and river water and perch and minnows they'd seine while wading in the clear, shallow water. Small lives flickered about their ankes, and the gold sand rasped the arches of their feet. It was nice to get your jeans soaked without Big Sister disapproving. It was nice to do nothing.

'Did you fish him out?'

'Huh?' Danny distinctly remembers telling this jerk that he didn't want to talk about it. It was a horrible sight and made him wonder what his father looked like under the ocean.

'Richard, my friend. Did you fish him out?'

He remembers the feel of moss winnowing the current,

and how he cringed into the wafting slime, and how a bit of fear peeped into his heart each time something sparkled from the moss into the channels, flashing silver into the net. He didn't want to step on frogs. There was something horrible in that, something human.

At sunset in the big river they'd string long, hundred-hook lines up and down the channels, sometimes in water up to their chests, and he'd cringe when he reached into the floating bait bucket, closing his hand in the turmoil of small, frantic fish around a perch. It strained, very alive and strong, in his fist. Then he'd hook it through the back so it would live to twitch gold and green in the moonlight to tempt big catfish.

'Forgive me. I forgot. You don't want to talk about it.'

'Right.'

'But I can't help it.'

There were snapping turtles and water moccasins and the immense, quiet peace, and he was glad of his grandfather's presence in the creeping dusk. And the insects, big African moths around the camp fire and praying mantises and crickets raging. He remembered how the insects would settle on his grandfather's khakis. He was that quiet. The old man looked at him once and saw he was squeamish about a big black grasshopper crawling up the shoulder of the khaki. He smiled at Danny, then fell asleep as the grasshopper crawled up to his collar, then fell asleep itself.

'You know how it is.'

Lester yawns and opens a beer. He should back off. Danny won't be pushed. Les must take his mind off the objective for a while, and since it's been a day since his encounter with Mary Ann, he lets his mind drift into the erotic. It's good cover. Mary Ann had been too easy.

Les liked a disciplined toying with emotion and sexuality

– something that pushed you to an edge. Something that opened you up, taught you something new. Who wants healthy, predictable sex? Animals can manage that.

But this Wendy had possibilities, despite her apparent wholesomeness. Maybe she rides a line between thrill seeking and normality. That's just using common sense. But there's some imagination under there. Some inner squigglies.

But at present Wendy's in love with Danny, Lester figures, and he can't afford to muddy the water if he's to get hold of the software case. To assuage himself beneath the boredom of the stars he uses Wendy's wet, erect nipples as a springboard to the past.

Boing.

The dark-haired girl looked smart. He drifts back.

'May I sit down?' she asked.

He nodded. He liked to let women think they manipulated him, and found that acting shy and intelligent worked best, unless they weren't smart enough to pick up on the intelligent part, which was sometimes the case in topless joints.

'You look serious.'

'High-minded.' He smiled. His eyes were coke-bright.

'So I noticed. Buy me a drink.'

He liked her straightforward manner. He bought a drink.

'Cheers,' she said. They drank. He handed her the vial. She disappeared into the bathroom.

'You're new in here.' She returned, eyes bright.

'I'm new in town.'

'You look like a cop.'

'I'm a poet. You shoot up?'

She watched him check the faint tracks on her arms, then smiled. 'How much you got?'

'Enough.'

'My girlfriend will have to come along.'

'Break my heart.'

'You're vile.' She smiled, handing him back the vial.

'Keep it. You6ve got a couple more dances to go.'

He wanted her to keep the vial. Why take chances? It wasn't like he didn't have a pile of the stuff. Before he'd quit, he'd stolen nine ounces from the evidence safe at the courthouse. The coke was his ticket to the bizarre – the bazaar of the bizarre.

They drank.

'What made you quit?' He liked it that she hasn't touched him yet; there was something refined in that. When he was coked up, he needed expert women, women quicker at fantasies than he. Women with cosmic sexuality. Emotional yet cold.

'Bored.'

'Being a cop? That's odd.'

'It's like sex. The actions are one thing, the spirit another. I got bored of being a bully.' He let that sink in. 'You never get to know anybody like that.'

'Mmmmm.' She looked at him, sucked on her straw.

He'd said a mouthful.

'Like sex clubs,' he continues. 'Clean, organized, sterile.'

'Got something against cleanliness?'

'Just organization. Let me have a snort.'

She handed him the vial. 'You're vile. But I know what you mean.'

'I bet you do.'

'Thank you.'

He took a big whiff from the back of his hand, and his scalp crawled.

He didn't like heroin users because they reminded him of his parents golfing. Nine holes a week did the trick. But Sugar was obviously into coke and speed. She liked to push it to the edge. Already he was imagining what they'd do to her friend, the tall, somnolent redhead. He could see her trembling.

You needed these contrasts.

'Nice car,' Sherry said in the parking lot.

On the way to the motel the two girls nestled next to him and smoked a joint, and he determined that they weren't being followed. Inside the motel room, they tossed their jackets on the bed, and Sugar grabbed the bottle of Scotch.

'I left the rigs in the car,' he lied. 'Be right back.'

Outside, he turned the corner to Room 217. Inside, he turned on the light, pulled back the bed, lifted the carpet free from the tack strip and revealed two sparkling ounces of Bolivian blue flake. He grabbed an ounce, dropped the rug, slid the bed back. Then, from underneath the sofa, he pulled out a carton of three hundred Plastipak syringes.

The girls were in the shower, but two spoons lay on the dressing table, their handles bent to level the bowls to hold water. He smiled. Primitive bitches. From his overnight bag he took a glass vial, which he rinsed with alcohol and distilled water, then tore open the sterile wrapping from needle and syringe, pulled the cap off the needle and drew up seventy cc's of distilled water. Then he cut open the ounce.

His knees weakened, and it took an effort to remind himself to wait for the girls. He swallowed, mixed up four hits, which dissolved instantly, mute testimony to the purity of the drug. He wanted it. But he pulled up another seventy cc's and made more hits. The first time he did a hit, he'd been frightened. But the idea was deliciously naughty, and he wanted a little depravity. Nothing else would've interested him.

It had been real good. The physical rush made you wonder why drugs didn't make people feel like this all the time. It was more relaxing than sniffing it and babbling and thinking.

This was the real thing. It was chilling and warm and universal and intimate and laid-back erotic and, no denying it, it was a little phallic. You'd been entered. There was an immediate taste in the back of your throat, and the sharp inrush of breath as an exotic animal grew inside you. There were no words.

His hand shook when he capped the needles.

'Jesus Christ,' whispered Sherry.

He tried to smile. She was tall with upturned breasts, butt smooth and high like a child's. If it weren't for the knowledge in her eyes, he would've thought her too young. She dropped the towel and gulped.

'Where'd you get all that?'

'God loves me. Have a seat.'

She slipped beside him, gawking like a kid. 'Can I have a hit?' she asked.

He continued drawing up hits, laying the individual syringes carefully on the desk table.

'I've never seen so many hits at once,' she breathed.

'I hate to stop to mix up another after I've started, don't you?'

'Right. Your hands shake.'

'Mine are shaking already.'

'I know what you mean. Smell it.'

'It's strong.'

'God.'

She folded her hands and pressed them between her thighs, watching him work.

'How do you know that's the right amount?'

'Practice.'

He pulled up two larger amounts into new syringes for himself and once again had trouble capping the last needle, his hands were shaking so. God, he was ready. But he was not going to spoil it by getting ahead of himself. Control.

Control. He couldn't be knocked-back rushing through a garden of earthly delights before the girls did it. They might split with the toot. But afterward they'd want to stay.

'What's Sugar doing?' he asked.

'She's probably coming.' Sherry giggled.

It always amazed him what this stuff could get you. 'You ready?' he asked Sherry, ready to give her the shot without Sugar in the room, wanting Sugar to walk in and see her longing, writhing.

'Sure.'

The door to the bathroom opened and Sugar walked in, wearing the shift she wore in the bar.

'Jesus Christ,' she said, looking at the big bag of cocaine.

'Ready?' he asked.

'Does Sammy Davis wear jewelry?'

'Will you do me, Sugar?' Sherry asked. She appeared younger, happy as a kid.

'Come here.'

The redhead hopped over to the smaller, dark-haired girl and wrapped her arms around her. Sherry giggled.

'Sit down.'

Their intimacy distracted Lester, and only the girl's weight on the bed brought him out of his reverie. Sugar stood in front of him.

'Hold her,' she said. 'Pump, honey.'

'Hurry.'

The needle lay flat against the stretched skin at the point where the lovely vein winnowed into the lower arm. Lester could feel his jaw tighten as the needle indented the tender flesh.

'Mmm,' she said.

'Got it. Ease up.'

Lester let go. Before it was halfway in, the redhead said,

'Jesus, that's so nice. So nice.' Sugar pushed it all the way in, and the redhead's nipples hardened.

'Thank you, baby.'

She withdrew quickly. Sherry licked her lips with eyes closed, leaned forward. Lester had an erection.

'Looks strong, Lester,' said Sugar. 'Let's hurry.'

'Do you want me to do you?'

She swallowed, nodded.

Sherry slid to the floor, took his hardness into her anxious, expert mouth. Sugar watched, pulling back the long red hair so he could see too.

'That's a good girl.'

'Do it there,' Sugar said. She pointed to the inside of her thigh.

He hit on the first try, and she said, 'That's good, keep it in for a minute. Oh, God. Where'd you get this stuff? Jesus. Pump it. I need to lie down.' But he left it in for a moment, forcing her to stand, impaled, straining to stand up under the thundering pleasure. 'Thank you,' she whispered.

She was beside him on the bed. Her chest arched, and her breath came fast, as though in orgasm.

'Hurry,' she whispered.

He did himself easily. Before the shot was all in, he tasted it and realized the incredible power of it, and the whole room started to shake. His vision blurred, and for a moment he wondered if he'd done too much. Matrons in starchy tennis skirts drifted across his parents' neat lawn. Then the animal awakened, and he knew it was all right. The driving sexual warmth spread through him and he knew how the world hungered for itself. Then he could think no more. He lay back, in love with the redhead's high, delicate cheekbones, the brunette's trembling hands in her hair.

9

'The room is registered to Hugo Daley. 1251 Live Oak. San Angelo, Texas.' David is looking through very dark sunglasses at the weird country outside of Truth or Consequences, New Mexico. He's in a phone booth listening to the voice of Manny Garcia, who used to be his cameraman until, thanks to Chuckles, he developed debilitating heterosexuality. Manny used to have artistry, a cold eye for hot detail, until his hands began to shake when he was filming a scene involving Chuckles. He started to drink. And actually tried to kiss her once. David bankrolled him, sent him away, hired another fag. Manny owes him. David has asked him to check out the registration in the La Quinta, where he had Chuckles's calls traced.

'Good, Manny. See you shortly. Stay away from that room. Get away immediately.' David hangs up, feeling certain that Manny will linger around the La Quinta like a sick dog and that Chuckles will spot him. San Angelo? Where the hell is that? 'Hand me that map, Chili.' He slides over in the backseat. 'Let's blow.' As they tear into the desert toward El Paso, David looks at the girls and thinks maybe he'd better get them some more conservative clothes. Or maybe they could masquerade as a funeral, he thinks, in the black Lincoln. You know – black veils, high heels, oral sex.

'You're nuts,' says Crisco. 'Saltwater taffy.'

* * *

Mary Ann bathes in West Texas twilight. Little Hugo lumbers about the backyard in a rubber-duck inner tube. A cordless phone rests by her lawn chair, and Lester's voice is still warm in her ear. Lester is bad, she can feel it. There's nothing left inside him, and this frees her to a river of sensation. He *makes* her do things. And it's him that's bad, not her. She doesn't want another warm, stupid, good person for a lover. All her good and warmth is used up on the Hugos. She needs a cold lover, so she can be cold back. This keeps the affair simple.

She remembers a night long ago, before she poked the cowpoke, before she realized she would have to pretend she loved someone forever, someone she didn't know. Before she was trapped. An evening right out of *Gatsby* – jonquil convertible, wind in the wisteria – with a boy from chemistry class pulling up in front of her dorm to take her out in the lush spring night. She had a ribbon in her hair and felt like she could be anything she wanted to be, there in the hallway of spring. It was like acting. She was free. She was no longer Mary Ann Carlisle sitting in high school, dutifully trembling and unsure, waiting for the cowpoke to notice her.

'Good evening,' said the boy.

'The good die young,' she'd quipped, her voice coming out of nowhere. And something had happened in his eyes. He hadn't expected this. He was happy. She sort of invented herself in his eyes. If one could lilt in one's walk, as one lilted in talk, she thought, she'd lilt down the steps. She could be anything she wanted. Anything.

The phone rings again and fear prickles her neck, wells in her tummy. Either way, Lester or Hugo, she's nervous. But it's a Yankee voice, someone who needs to drop off something for Hugo.

* * *

'Okay, Hugo, pay attention.' Chuckles has Hugo sitting in the armchair in the La Quinta. She's on the bed. 'We're not watching any more of those damn videos. There's something wrong with them. They're sick anyway. Save your money. Work hard. Go to heaven. Blah, blah, blah. Jesus. But I mean they're sicker than even that. Somebody's done something. When was the last time you got horny in church? Don't answer that. Did you know one of those TV Bible pounders wears a codpiece? Never mind. Look, Hugo, I know you want to help me. Improve me. That's sweet. But fuck you. I'll take care of myself. Okay?'

'Sure, Chuckles, you can do anything you want. It's a free country.' He looks sad.

Chuckles feels like petting him. It's sick. 'Look, Hugo. Let's talk about chemical warfare, okay?'

'Okay.'

'You know how much money they spend on that stuff?'

'No.'

'A lot. More in one day than you'll make in ten lifetimes.'

'Damn.'

'They figure out chemicals to make people feel bad.'

'To make Communists feel bad.'

'Okay, Communists. What if they tried to make 'em feel good?'

'Why?'

Little Hugo answers the door in his rubber-duck inner tube. Before him stands a man in sunglasses. Mary Ann wonders why he's wearing sunglasses at sunset. Maybe it makes the colors deeper, or maybe he's been to the optometrist, had his pupils dilated. That's a painful thing.

'Are you Mrs Hugo Daley?'

'Yes, I am. Come over here, Hugo.'

Little Hugo does his pogo-stick routine, hopping around his mother as she moves forward.

'I called earlier. Could you give these papers to Hugo, please?'

'Certainly. Come in.'

'Thanks. It's been a long drive.'

David steps inside hesitantly. He fumbles with his brief-case, looks awkward.

'Here. Sit at the table. Coffee?'

'No thanks. I'm in a hurry.'

Mary Ann floats to the surface of a clear glass egg, filled with waves of pink and azure and green. Angelfish rise with her; some sink. A creature with Technicolor tentacles caresses her rubbery, floating limbs. She is distantly aware she can't breathe, but somehow she doesn't care.

'Look at this. Look at this.'

Her eyes stretch open to see a TV, placed at an angle above her bed like TVs in the hospital. She's afraid there's been a car wreck. Oh, God. Little Hugo. She jerks up. But she's bound or in traction. Scared.

'You like your TV, honey?' It's a female voice, faintly Negro. 'We fixed it up there special for you. We can't have you looking around, so we kinda had to fix your head and the tube in the same dimension – if you get my drift. This was my idea. Some folks were for keeping you in the dark. Say thank you.'

Mary Ann's tongue is too thick to move. She can move her head only half an inch to each side. A big fish sucks at her stomach. She's sick.

'Calm down, honey. You got nothing left to throw up.'

Little Hugo is dangled upside down before her. Squawking but obviously alive.

'Here he is, the fat little son of a bitch. Look quick. He's heavy.'

Little Hugo is lifted up, away to somewhere behind her. Fear like cold water spreads through her.

Then she's blindfolded. Her arms are tied to the bed. She feels a light pinch on the inside of her elbow. Then it all gets warm. Comfy.

She sleeps.

Chuckles looks at Hugo sleeping. Like a giant panda, those sad, Chinese bears that won't make babies in the zoo. They have some sense. Why bring a baby into a trap? Or Tijuana? Or Beverly Hills? Or Oakland, to Chuckles's old apartment. Why not? After her third stepfather she got the hang of it. She learned what her mother meant when she said. 'You can get him, baby. You trick that bastard into taking care of your mommy. Don't let him near me. Not an inch. You fuck him out of that money. Give me a kiss.'

She remembers the routine. Waiting for the man at the bottom of the steps. Dressed up like Shirley Temple for the occasion. You made your eyes big, too, like you were a doll, and talked sugary.

'Hi, Daddy. Let's get out of here. Mommy's in a state. Poor thing. I sure have missed you.'

'Hey, baby.'

It had all come from being quiet and watching. Listening. She hardly spoke before she was five. By then she'd copied a bunch of personalities. Knew how they worked and on whom. Most of them were her mother's, who seemed bored with just one. Her favorite was the Lauren Bacall, when her mama leaned against the doorjamb with a cigarette, eyebrows suggestively elevated, hip cocked.

'Good work, baby. Hurry next door. Dale's coming over. Give me a kiss.'

* * *

David is ashamed of himself: kidnapping women and children. He's never had to kidnap a woman before. He's low. Chuckles is low. Did she hurt his pride, is that it? He'd watched his parents kill each other with jealousy and swore he'd never practice that ignoble form of real estate himself. You got jealous because you were afraid, insufficient, a leech. But now he'd fallen into it, and look what it got him. The kid wanted to play Spin the Couch all morning. David doesn't know how to handle this. The idea was to get Hugo to cough up Chuckles, in return for his wife and son. But there's a weak spot: what if he doesn't want his disgusting family?

Meanwhile David has movie contracts to fulfill.

'Parcel for Mr Daley.'

Hugo looks at the bellhop. It's nice to have bellhops. He could never understand why people complained about motels. He takes the package, signs for it and tips the guy a quarter. 'Thanks, bud.'

It's a video.

'Oh, God,' says Chuckles.

Inside the package is a note. 'Top secret,' it says. 'For your eyes only.'

Hugo is pleased. Secret company business. He's gained their confidence, he's moving up.

'Look, Chuckles. I'm supposed to look at this one by myself. Why don't you go down to breakfast and I'll be along in a flash.' Chuckles looks at him strangely.

'Don't hurt yourself,' she says.

Chuckles imagines a clean-cut executive expounding the virtues of desk tidiness while Hugo rolls around in the champagne bottles with an erection, uncontrollably aroused while Herman looks on. It's fairly disgusting. Halfway down the hall she stops, goes back and puts her ear to the door.

'Hi, Hugo. I guess you can see us. They're taking a movie of us. You can see we're all right. Little Hugo is fine. But they want that girl. You better bring her. Or something. I think they'd hurt us. But we're okay. It doesn't matter what you've been doing, I forgive you. Just come get us. There'll be further instructions later. We've had it if you call the cops. Don't do that, please don't.'

Chuckles hears weeping through the motel door, first the woman's, then Hugo's big soft sobs. She turns and walks down the hall.

David's after her. A quick glee at how much he must hurt runs through her tummy, but then she saddens. It's all so desperate, this love thing. She gave him his freedom, why can't he give her hers?

People handle their aloneness in different ways, thinks Danny. It's like flying a kite, a combination of letting go and pulling back. But Lester's all restraint. Lester is real alone. But you can't be all stifling warmth either. It's a fine line.

Danny wants to walk over to where Wendy dabbles in the river and hug her and not have the feeling of desolation Lester gives him. But something holds him back. Cuddling Wendy would sort of shut Lester out, and there's a code that Danny should pay attention to this guy who bought them beer and whose friend was just killed and who's just trying to be friendly. That would be impolite. You don't just go around sucking up all the cuddles you can get, do you? He remembers all the sort of hugging that went on in the sixties and remembers back to when it was the Autumn before the Summer of Love, back when Boston looked like the Joan Baez Drill Team.

Danny was as far away from Texas as he could get, yet felt

that he'd merely swapped bouffant and bubble gum for straight hair and granny glasses. Everyone was so ethereal, he could weep. How do you talk to these earnest people? He'd sent for Kim, his gamin high-school sweetheart, much his junior, much against his better judgement, such as it was – LSD based. Parking meters wiggled in the sunlight, and you wouldn't see little Kim staring vacuously into space, strumming a guitar and getting blandly cosmic. Most of those types looked like they'd be driving ranch wagons in a few years or looking worldly around the club pool.

In the Autumn before the Summer of Love, the startling sunlight plays hoochy-coo on the Charles River, and through the bright leaves Danny feels the dance of hoofbeats of Eurasian Steppes horsemen, the whisper of Egyptian priests, the tittering of field mice and girls and blood and children and stars. Somewhere people are reading the Tibetan *Book of the Dead* and lighting candles like mutant altar boys. Danny could weep.

But he's out of Texas. He's away from his mother and her cancer and her brand-new marriage to the up-and-coming congressman. He doesn't have to ride in the back of convertibles in parades of spit-licking Democrats. He's into LSD and ego loss and wants to turn his life into many lives, each a three-dimensional mosaic kaleidoscope. Ephemeral, real ephemeral. Noble and fun.

His mother is not leaning across the breakfast table, pulling open the nightgown, revealing the twisted white scar where her cancerous breast had been. She is not saying, 'You helped him do this to me. You might as well have done it yourself.' He is not seeing that beautiful, funny, crazy, strong woman going to pieces, his funny mommy.

He is not seeing how impossible it is for people to see each other, to get along. He's into LSD and overcoming things like jealousy that trap everybody; he wants to turn his life into many lives, and Kim arrives and they take lots of acid and they even have orgies, and Danny's love for the little girl is suddenly increased. She is not a small person. She is strong and adventurous.

Yet one night, when the walls are melting and emeralds are dripping from the ceiling, she tells him that before she came to Boston, her mother stood in front of the dresser mirror with a pistol and shot herself in the temple and left a note saying it was Kim's fault for not giving her a birthday card. And this casts a pallor on the evening. It does. Danny's obviously her only security. Some security, he thinks. No wonder she's so agreeable. She's scared to death. She wasn't doing it because she was into it. There is a deep quiet. Doves fall from trees like leaves. They do. And Kim takes a walk in the silence.

Danny is staring in stunned silence at the wall. She leaves. People in another room are doing something else. Years pass, and then Kim is falling through the door. The side of her little head is caved in, and she is whimpering 'Mommy, Mommy, Mommy,' and the floor is wiggling and there is lots of blood. Someone caved in the side of her head with a club when she wouldn't blow him in an alley. She's covered with her own shit. The emergency room melts. After her skull and brain surgery she's a little insecure. She has no father and she's wondering about her relationship with Danny. You can see she wants a little security. 'Are you my brother?'

'No.'

'Lyndon Johnson?'

The Winter before the Summer of Love is a cold one. Ice runs halfway up the hubcaps of their three-hundred-dollar hearse in a narrow drive between ramshackle apartments on Pleasant Street. Kim has become a small, brittle child. Danny is spending his life in guilt. She is clairvoyant. His stomach tightens up thirty seconds before she begins to cry, two rooms away. She weeps if he even thinks of another woman. She sees a shrink. She comes home early from the shrink and catches Danny with the upstairs neighbor, and Kim knocks out glass in the windows and rakes her wrists across the brilliant shards.

'Let's get married,' says Danny. 'Right away.'

It takes Danny two days to chop the hearse out of the ice with a construction pick. He can feel Kim staring down at him through the high window. She was once a spirited urchin who got a kick out of getting out of control. He'd felt for a brief time that love might not necessarily end up stifled, controlled, trapped in a straitjacket. Sure, everybody's jealous, but you ought to control that shit. Give freedom: a nice gift. That's what he'd been looking for. Freedom in a woman. Good thinking. Her eyes are as big as planets.

They're taking the hearse home to Texas, but driving through the South en route. Danny figures he can get a taste of the highway, get some magnolias and Spanish moss and the rich poverty of the black South to offset the chill of the last few months. There's some mystery down there anyway. The Boston accent has grown abrasive, the people coarse, the snow dirty. And going home to be married to a spooky basket case makes any detour welcome. His neck chills and he looks up. She's smiling at him.

You can't turn the hearse off once it's started. The compression is too low. You have to sit for three hours while the engine cools. So they drive nonstop from Boston to north Carolina, a relaxing little jaunt, and spend the first night in a trailer park in rain so bad, they don't even step outside. She wants to make love, such as it is, inside the cloying purple drapes with a tiny light on. She says she must be able to see into his eyes.

'Oh, Daddy,' she sighs. 'Daddy. Daddy.'

In a trailer park in Macon, the transmission falls out.

'Man is burdened by his possessions,' Danny explains to Kim when he leaves everything but their overnight bags in the hearse and hits the highway with his thumb out. She's good bait and they score a ride to Atlanta immediately. Kim fixes the big redneck with coquettish eyes, talks about D. H. Lawrence and sexual mysticism and experiments with a Marlene Dietrich laugh for fifty miles.

'I never knew ol' Lawrence said all that,' their chauffeur comments. 'But he sure ran a hell of a race at Daytona last year, 'fore his engine blew.'

Then it is the Spring before the Summer of Love and Danny is on a plane to Los Angeles, a flight heading west thirty-five minutes after Kim's flight heads east to an asylum in Ohio. Talk about a close one. It feels like his stomach is hurtling east. Somehow he's found two thousand dollars left him from his father's death and he's going to LA to become a dealer so he can travel and have fun and put a few more miles between himself and Marlene Dietrich. Guido picks him up at the airport in a black '55 Dodge, and the ocean and the sunshine smell fine, and the palm trees along Sepulveda guide him out of the cold mask of winter. He's young again. So when the weed isn't immediately available, the backup acid deal in San Francisco seems fine.

'Sure, man. I've never been to San Francisco.'

Well, it doesn't happen like that. He and Guido leave the two grand with Sandy and beat it to the beach with the surfboard, and driving back in the late afternoon, a couple of goddesses are hitchhiking in bikinis, and at three o'clock in the morning Danny senses the ray of a flashlight probing his nakedness, and the girl's face is illuminated beneath him by yet another flashlight, and it is apparent they are surrounded by police above the ocean in San Pedro. Guido and the other girl struggle up from the backseat.

'Don't you kids know there's a curfew?'

Nobody knows.

'How old are you girls?'

Nobody knows.

One cop takes Guido and Danny to the patrol car while the other stays with the chicks and discovers the sour cream container full of reefer, and they handcuff Danny and Guido – arrest them, in fact – and search the trunk and find a book bag full of bi-phetamines, and everybody goes downtown. Danny's teeth are grinding. What a time to be awake. All night grilling.

Chuckles sits in the La Quinta Coffee Shop practicing her Madonna, her Tina Turner, and for a lark she gives the big sidewalk window a taste of Jane Fonda and Olivia Newton-John. Nobody notices. Bad day. Hardened Texans, city dwellers. What is this, little Manhattan?

What's she gonna do about Hugo? David is seriously chasing her. That's beautiful. So he's kidnapped Hugo's wife? Little Hugo? She laughs. Poor David, the idiot. Here comes Hugo, looking like a pallbearer. He couldn't keep a straight face if he tried.

'Hi, Chuckles.'

'Peeky, pooky, Hugo. How was the video?'

'All right.'

'Hot new stuff?'

'No. It was business.'

'Looks like sad business.'

'I'm just tired.'

'Of me?'

'Oh, no, Chuckles. I like you.'

'Sure.'

Hugo looks hurt. God, he's confused.

'What you having?' Food has become a big conversation piece with Chuckles and Hugo. It's filling the void left by football.

10

Danny and Lester have returned to the Liberty Bell Motel to continue drinking. Danny has quit on the beer and is into the reliable Jack Daniel's, the lovely brown whiskey, the joyous amber, the impeccable bite, the love of his life.

The ten o'clock news from the TV is the only light in the room, and Danny studies the weird shadows the flickering glow casts on Lester's face. Lester's getting a little drunk now, and Danny likes him better for it. The guy was too together earlier, you know, for Danny's taste. If you're not a little tattered and tarnished at the psychic edges, you ain't shit. Danny's tattered himself pretty good. He loves his Jack Daniel's. It is the best thing in the whole gooey world, maybe even the universe, and for sure in Room 16, since Wendy's back at the river smoking an itty-bitty doobie.

On TV a big Mexican is being led out of a pink trailer in handcuffs. The cops are marching him through an ocean of crying children, and his wife is holding another child and crying, and the cops let the big guy stop to hold one of his sons in farewell, and suddenly the big guy spins around and the stomach of the cop on the right opens like a bad dream and his guts plop out and he has a very startled, silly expression, and it seems the cameraman is torn between focusing on the expression or the bursting intestines, for the camera jerks crazily back and forth between the dangling entrails and the face in close-up, and you don't see the big

Mexican again until he's chopped apart by what must be at least a .45. He is slammed against the squad car, and great chunks of his skull and brains flap into the crowd, and the cop just won't quit shooting. An arm is blown off, and the whole side of the car is dripping fingers and flesh, and the cop shoots him forever.

'That's why those steering wheels on cholo mobiles are so small,' says Lester. 'So Mexicans can drive handcuffed.'

Black humor is a necessary ingredient in Danny's life, and he has great respect for it in almost all forms. Lester has amazed him. 'Jesus Christ,' he says.

'That was the fucker that killed my friend.'

'Speedy trial.

'A real tax-saver.'

Danny doesn't feel too good. It reminds him of Otto. There'd never been anybody who looked more like a West Texas cowboy than Otto, and he was from Maryland. Danny's only partner, and Danny didn't approve of partners. But after he blew up four hundred pounds of pot and almost blew himself up with it, Danny figured he was getting too shaky to go it alone. He needed someone to watch his back. Then he'd get back on the road.

He remembers the motel room where Otto brought him breakfast that morning. They'd been up all night snorting speed with a couple of apprentice smuggleresses who were taking four suitcases of pot on a two A.M. flight from El Paso to Pittsburgh. They were showing them how smugglers lived hard and fast because the next day they might be dead or in jail. They were a couple of true professors and at about one-thirty they patted them one last time on their amphetamine-jumpy bottoms and sent them to the airport, extremely pleased that it wasn't Danny or Otto drifting into the twisted night.

But the girls came right back, eyes as big as stars, rather pissed off.

'How much weight is in these things?'

'The usual.'

'Bullshit.'

Each suitcase weighed thirty pounds, the same as six others Danny and Otto had flown out that very week. But the girls didn't believe them. The three hours of heart-pounding, nipple-stiffening, skin-chilling doses of ether-based Methedrine had finally spooked then, and they were heavily into Methedrine psychosis and seemed not only frightened but actually distrustful.

'Keep away from our house. It's hot. And the airport's hot too. Come on, Happy.'

They looked pretty intense, and as they huffed it out of there, little hips twitching haughtily, Danny thought they might as well stay the rest of the night, practice a little more. But no, they'd made like wet beavers and split. It was bad.

Otto had to be in San Antonio the next morning, and Danny had flown in and out of the same airport so much that he was practically on a first-name basis with airport security. He didn't want to do it again. Even though the pickup had a false bottom, they needed the girls' garage to load in. Now they couldn't do that. He was stuck with a couple of suitcases and an amphetamine-whiskey hangover.

'Give me a drink,' he said.

'You need to eat,' observed Otto, but he handed Danny the Jack Daniel's and took off. While he was gone, Danny consulted what was left of his intuition. No help. It didn't seem fair. Drive the Sierra Blanca emigration checkpoint with two full suitcases in full view? Forget that. The minute he got charitable, tried to create a few jobs for the common folk, the shit hit the fan. No good deed goes unpunished.

But then he thought how cute the girls looked learning

how to be smugglers, twisting around naked on the motel bed, and he got a teeny bit of guilt. Guilt was terrible luck. He was a mess.

Otto came back with eggs and sausage that looked like elephant scabs, and Danny ate and felt better. They had another drink and laughed, but Danny was still trembling. Staying up all night taking stimulants made him paranoid, even if he didn't do anything naughty. And the tendency was to keep whiffing, because of the incredible sexual tinglings which, at the moment, made it all seem worthwhile. But the food helped, and Otto had a calming effect. He seemed particularly calm and rational that morning. He didn't have to drive.

'Calm down,' said Otto, chopping up another line. 'Them chicks was just wired.'

Danny looked at the motel ceiling thinking he must have set a record for motel ceilings, the kind that wiggled anyway. He shouldn't do anything today, that much was obvious. His job was to get fucked up so he could go to sleep. Get sane. He was good at getting fucked up. It was part of his job.

'Let's get out of here. Who knows what?' muttered Danny.

They dropped off the suitcase at a different motel, and Danny changed sunglasses and they ducked into a bar.

'That'll fool 'em,' said Otto.

The twelfth whiskey cheered him up, and somewhere around Oklahoma City he sobered up. Then he remembered throwing up all over the Border Patrol's feet at the checkpoint. With puke on his pants and shoes, the cop didn't even look at the suitcases. You must play these things off the cuff, Danny told himself, and trust your intuition. As he dropped a couple of quarters into the Magic Fingers massage that night and poured himself the tiniest of evening cocktails, he told himself he'd done just fine. Walls rose up to protect the pure of heart.

* * *

100

Wendy wonders why she likes Danny. The waters of the Llano River curl by her ankles as she dangles her feet from the granite ledge. There's not much solid about him, and he's back at the motel talking to Lester, somebody she can tell he doesn't like much. He's gonna get his lights punched out with that smart-ass attitude. What's he think he's proving? She feels Mindy the Yorkshire terrier nuzzle her hand. A weird little dog. The only thing worse than an ungroomed Yorkshire terrier is a well-groomed Yorkshire terrier.

She thinks about rain, the pictures of moisture cycles in her eighth-grade science text. Is it possible that this water washing her calves was the same water she waded in, years ago, in California? Maybe you can't step in the same river twice, but what about waters? Different rivers, same waters?

Wendy goes back to the Liberty Bell and watches the weird shadows from the TV on the cheap motel drapes. It is cool now, a touch of autumn in the air. She isn't anxious to go into the room. She doesn't want to hear Danny and Lester work on each other. She hopes Danny's asleep and that Lester has gone away. But she checks the parking lot and there's Lester's Toyota. Damn. At least there's only one of him. She opens the door and sees Danny asleep on the bed, the bottle of Jack Daniel's within reach. Then she sees Lester going through her duffel bag.

'What are you doing?' This is her excuse to get rid of him, she realizes, but she's also frightened. There's something cold about him.

'Looking for matches,' he says without flinching, without getting out of her duffel bag. She doesn't remember him smoking. Her neck chills.

'Here.' She tosses him her matches. 'What do you smoke?'

'I don't. But I thought I'd borrow your bathroom before I left, and sometimes burning a little match in there afterward

. . . you know, helps. I didn't want to leave a bad impression.'

'Hurry up. I'd like to go to bed.'

Lester sits on the pot trying not to laugh, making farting noises with his lips. He goes through all the motions: flushes the toilet, lights matches, washes his hands. Action, he loves it. What a life. Just as Wendy walked in, his hand had been closing around a plastic software case. Luck of the Irish. He'd almost had it, and soon he *would* have it. 'There's no business like show business,' he sings. 'Like no business I know.' He dries his hands and fakes a stumble when he walks out the door.

'Wow. I'm drunker than I thought. Ol' Dan there can sure put it away.'

'Practice, practice.'

'I better not drive.'

'Get a room. We need sleep.'

'Perhaps I should get a room.' This girl doesn't seem to like him. How very unfair. What's he done, huh? Been a pleasant fellow. Bought beer. Made nice conversation. Told jokes. Welcome to Texas, sweetheart. Fluff up or maybe ol' Les will turn the charm on you. Bring out the real you. How'd you like that, sweetness?

'Have a nice sleep,' he offers on the way out. 'Sweet dreams.'

He gets a room. He dreams. It's the same old dream. The Cong have his friend Max tied to a tree. They're forcing Lester to watch as they cut Max's pecker into half-inch strips, which they dangle in front of Max's eyes and then feed to him. Make him chew every bite like a good boy. Every time Lester closes his eyes, they pull out one of his fingernails. It's a great game. Soon Lester sees the absolute humor in it. It's like a party, yes it is. Cher gets her nails done. Yoko Ono flies to Paris. All Maxy has to do is chew. 'Chew, Maxy, chew!' shouts Les. 'Chew for Cher's new fruit knives! Chew for Yoko's Swiss poodle!'

Danny continued bouncing between the East Coast and the Rio Grande twice, sometimes three times a week, forgetting what he wanted other than the fear, which meant he was alive, and the speed and darkness, which meant he was going somewhere. The bucks kept stacking up, and ladies loved the outlaw, or at least his cocaine. The only thing that saved him from terminal wealth was how much fun it took to relax. He delighted in showing up at the homes of uptight gangsters, loose, twitchy bitches hanging on his arms, coke falling from his pockets. Just to piss 'em off. What kind of outlaws were these guarded little types? Corporation guys.

Since he was getting too bent to drive, he hired drivers, flew around in airplanes, had forty pairs of sunglasses and rented three or four motel rooms in the same town. It made sense. One for the money. Two for the toot. Three for the chicks. And four, if it was a dull day, for business. One day he woke up confused in a hotel, wearing only his bathrobe, forty grand in the pocket, unable to remember how he got there or what town he was in. But he gave the girl a thousand dollars to give the guy down the hall a blowjob in exchange for a pair of pants, only the trousers were too big and he had to tie the pants up with a chain he ripped out of the toilet. Things were warping out of control, but Otto came and saved him. Two thousand miles. They burst into a plush men's store, Danny barefoot and shirtless, and spent three thousand dollars in twenties and bought a shoe-shine boy twelve pairs of shoes. At the height of his popularity the Mexicans fronted him four hundred pounds on top of the four hundred he bought. This was a grand new thing.

That night they nailed one of his trucks at the checkpoint.

Four hundred pounds. His four hundred. The Mexicans explained that the fronted load got through. It was the four hundred he'd paid for that was unfortunately confiscated by the cops. It was his karma, they explained. And it was also his job to sell the four hundred that got through, as he'd agreed. They'd had a vision – God was rough on uncool gringos.

'You hear about the Mexican coyote?' he asked.

'No, Danny.'

'Chewed off three paws and still got caught in the trap.'

'You hear about the gringo who locked his keys in the car?'

'No.'

'Took him three days to get his family out.'

They knew where his family lived. He had to sell their four hundred, and they got all of his connections from Otto. Danny couldn't buy lunch.

Otto went to work for them, but he liked to have fun too. A month later Danny got a two A.M. phone call.

'Pick me up in the ditch behind the 7–11 on Redwood and Ben White.'

Danny's headlights showed nothing as they drifted through the autumn weeds, and his nuts were crawling up around his ears. Otto sounded scared, and it was hard to think of him scared. Somebody was trying to kill him, most likely. Some humorless type. He was slammed into the dirt, a great weight on his back, hot breath in his ear. When Otto was finally convinced it was Danny, he let him up. Except for his cowboy boots, which were stuffed with money, the big guy was naked.

'Turn off those lights,' he whispered.

Otto'd been awake for a week, and after tying a bartender and a stripper together in the sixty-nine position, he'd become convinced he was being followed, watched, tricked and waited for by bad guys or narcs at the trailer, so he'd taken off his clothes, because he thought he was too twisted to empty the pockets of all the stray drugs effectively. As they stood inside the trailer, finally safe, Danny looked at Otto all trembling and sheepish and was proud to know him.

'What were you after in that ditch, Otto?'

'A gopher. It could gopher my pants.'

Otto didn't want to risk waking up his old lady, so Danny tiptoed into the bedroom and, while he teased open the drawer, realized Otto's big, trembling hands would've shaken the dresser like a rattle. Somehow Danny felt wise and jolly walking down the hall with Otto's pants. The only way to get free of the tension was to do something crazy.

Back in the living room, Otto was chopping up a line eleven or thirteen inches long. He nodded at Danny to toss his pants by the chair and kept chopping, his big jaws clenched, his teeth grinding. His .357 rested in its usual place on the tacky coffee table. To impress his admirers Otto had developed a little trick he called Polish Roulette. Played like Russian Roulette but with only one chamber empty. His trick, however, was to leave the chamber next to the barrel empty, so that when he placed the gun to his head and pulled the trigger, the empty chamber revolved into the barrel and the firing pin came down on air. Click. After a moment of suspense the startled admirer could see nothing but big ugly .357 slugs in the exposed chambers. Otto would laugh and put the gun back on the table.

He reached into the wad of money in his boots and pulled out a fifty, rolled it, and, in spite of the fact that he was strung out and needed a snort badly, leaned back in his chair, smiled through clenched teeth and handed Danny the bill. Danny snorted, handed it back. After his snort Otto relaxed. Some of the anxiety left his eyes.

'Thanks for picking me up, Bubba,' he said.

'You probably ought to sleep.' Danny laughed.

Otto laughed. Then he put the .357 to his temple and blew his brains all over Danny's shirt.

A miscalculation.

The next day, after the business with the cops, when Grenda was at her mother's, Danny went out to clean the carpet and scrub the walls. Talk about picking a guy's brains. And now he had no one to play with.

Lester trembles. Max's pecker is completely missing. Where it was looks like the cavity for a wisdom tooth, and the gooks are turning around, coming at Les like a platoon of manic Benihana chefs. He tries to wake up but can't. He's sweating. The jungle is like some polyester fern bar on mushroom and amphetamines, closing in, too much hair spray, too much cologne, too many salesmen. The gooks are now carrying knives and briefcases filled with stock options and deeds to Malibu real estate and IRA accounts. The plants are growing like mad, and vines wrap around his neck, squalling newborn children in each leaf. A huge cypress groans. Its bark splits open, spilling forth camel guts, and miniature Michael Jacksons dance out selling Pepsi and small statues of Jehovah.

The door to his room is pounding. His neck is paralyzed. He has to wake up to live. He is surrounded by his mother's bridge club. They are chatting, chatting, chatting, chatting. He has to wake up.

'Wake up!'

Someone is shaking him.

'Wake up!'

Danny is standing over him. 'Wake up, you asshole.'

11

Hugo doesn't want Chuckles to hear him doing push-ups. She is snoring softly on the motel bed, and he feels kind of silly. He hasn't even dreamed about the tomato in days, yet he's been neglecting his push-ups. At home, with Mary Ann, if he even went one day without his workout, the whole ceiling of his bedroom would turn tomato-red in the darkness and he couldn't sleep. Or if he did sleep, he'd get the tomato nightmare for sure.

A tomato so heavy he couldn't lift it would press down slowly on his chest and begin to decompose, getting all juicy and rotten, and his skin would get juicy and rotten, and pretty soon he and the tomato would mix together and drip down into the deep fungus of earth, and loam would fill his lungs and worms wiggle and chew through his brain. He would try to scream, but his throat would be packed with garbage, decomposing chipmunks, old toys and banana peels.

Bottles of three-dollar champagne litter the La Quinta carpet.

One tomato, two tomato. He has, on occasion, passed a little gas during calisthenics, and this worries him. How embarrassing in front of your new girlfriend.

Herman has sneaked out of the bathroom window and around the window ledge, on to the front porch and back into the room through the bedroom window, and lumbered back on to the bed beside Chuckles. Herman is watching Hugo disdainfully.

Eight tomato.

The cat waddles closer to the edge of the bed. Now its eyes are parallel with Hugo's as he rises.

Twelve tomato. The cat is laughing at him. He's certain. He closes his eyes. Fifteen tomato.

To help him through his exercises he often imagines the hard cinder track of his youth. Though he'd been big, he ran a hell of a quarter mile. Purely on guts. Give me all the goddamn pain you can, he'd tell himself. He can see the track beneath him, feel the reassuring *thud, thud, thud* of his feet as he muscled his way past more lithesome, graceful runners. *Thud. Thud. Thud.* The cat's claws dig into his back. He feels like he's covered by a forty-pound caterpillar.

But you don't stop Hugo, cat.

Nineteen tomato, twenty.

Baby Chili looks morosely out over the flat Houston wasteland and laughs. Some adventure. It's not the life she'd counted on with David. She's on the little Hugo detail and jealously listens to the snap, snap of the cards in the next room, where Crisco and David are playing gin. They've got the TV on too. Game shows. Don't they have cable out here?

Little Hugo is pushing a tractor around the carpet, making horrible noises. He sounds like a constipated Tasmanian devil. She flops into the chair, opens a *Lady's Home Journal* and stares over the top of it at Crisco and David. She envies that tall bitch's willowy height. How do they say it – a tall, cool one? More like a hot coal in a freezer. Miss Control. Miss Uppity. Tigress. Baby Chili can't remember her childhood, and that's not so long ago. She remembers the Walt Disney film, though, on jungles. *The Jungle Book*. There was a tiger in that. She'd imagined that's what her home looked like. Jungle. But she was not a tiger. Crisco was a tiger. Baby Chili was a little rabbit or something. Scared a lot.

Little Hugo runs the tractor over her feet, and she feeds him a phenobarbital.

Hugo looks out over Houston. He can see the ship channel from Lester's office window. He likes the tall buildings with Shell and Tenneco and Gulf signs on top, like Christmas baubles. The other buildings are gray and boring. He'd like a big neon tomato up on one. A red tomato that reads 'Hugo,' like he was an oil company. Hugo Oil. He could leave little Hugo an empire, like J.R. was going to leave to John Ross. But those people weren't very happy, and he was starting to mess up, just like them – everybody running away or tricking each other or kidnapping somebody. Just as he was getting successful. He sees Mary Ann again, tied to that bed. Who were these people? Why did they want Chuckles? And what did he do to deserve this?

He'd poked Chuckles, that's what. A lot. And worse than that, he loved her. In the old days you just loved somebody no matter what. You didn't poke other people because you might fall in love with them too. That was bad. His mother and father made it to the nursing home without that sort of complication. There's something tidy in that. Some love is bad. Is that it? You make a deal, like a business, and stick to it. Right?

He's sick with fear. Thrown up twice today.

All he can do is wait.

Chuckles lies on the bed with Herman watching the video on real estate investment. He's a West Texas boy, earnest as a preacher and real energetic. He's thumping a podium and Chuckles is getting horny. She freezes the picture. Stares at it. The guy has his mouth open. You can see his molars, his cavities. He's wearing a dumb tie. He's about as sexy as a washing machine. She's not horny anymore. She starts it up. Soon she's getting twitchy.

It's something in these tapes, she figures. There's something underneath them. Something good but tricky.

Crisco looks down at Mary Ann. She's a pretty thing. Fragile yet kind of hard. A ranch girl, a clean Texas cowgirl. My, my. Jessica Lange. Sleeping so comfy. Like a baby. How does my baby like the naughty heroin? Is it nice? You bet it is. Naughty baby. She likes it. Crisco can tell.

Shall we do up the baby a little cocaine, too, make her panties get all wet, or would that be naughty? That would make the clean girl think about naughty things she might like. That would make Crisco a naughty girl.

She lifts the sheets and peeks.

Hugo can't get it up. There is a horrible feeling – weak and frightened and empty – all through his body. He can't even do a push-up. He can't smile. He can't eat. But he can drink a little. But sour mash now. No more Mr Bubbly. He's brought in the heavy artillery. Chuckles sits by the bed in the chair, reading something. Hugo stares at the ceiling and waits for the phone to ring.

'Let's go out, Hugo. I'll show you some things.'

'I can't, Chuckles. You go ahead.'

'When are you going to tell me what's wrong? If I get bored, I'll split.'

Hugo stares at the ceiling. He can see little Hugo falling down a deep well. Falling and falling. *Ploosh.* He hits bottom way down in the dark. Then it sounds like a cat drowning. Someone's nailed Hugo's feet to the floor so he can't jump in. After a few gurgles there is silence. Mary

Ann's face appears – haunted, accusing. She won't say a word. Not a word.

'Look, Hugo. I know what the deal is. I listened by the door. Those kidnappers won't do anything. I know the main guy. He's harmless. I can handle him. Now cheer up.'

'Huh?'

Energy floods his soul, his body. 'You what?'

'He's in love with me. I'll handle it.'

'I want to know what you're after.' Danny looks at Lester across the breakfast table. Wendy is lighting a rare cigarette.

Lester's drinking coffee. He almost chokes but smooths it over. 'After?'

'After.'

Lester thought it was nice of Danny to wake him up during his nightmare. This was further evidence of simpleminded generosity. But now Danny's on dangerous ground.

'We were doing some work together. The cops didn't find it. I wondered if you picked it up. A software case. I'm sorry I rifled your stuff. You were asleep when I remembered.'

'Why didn't you ask?'

'I was having fun. It's not important. Thanks again for waking me up.'

'You were howling. What's that from?'

'The usual. You don't want to hear it.'

'A hero, huh?'

'Yep.'

'I don't want to hear it.'

'How'd you know it was me screaming?'

'You were the only other person in the place, besides that old guy, the manager. He's nearly deaf.'

'Right.'

'What were you working on?'

'Adapting subliminal effects to videotapes.'

'That's tricky.'

'Yep.'

'So what's the big secret?'

'Security.'

'Security?'

'It's a trade secret. You know, something you find out first and keep secret so other people can't use it. So you can make the money. Security. Haven't you seen all those cops around IBM buildings and stuff? They even have locks on their wastebaskets. To protect trade secrets. Get it?'

'Security sounds like a lot of work.'

'It is.'

Lester sops up egg yolk with wheat toast. His hangover is going away and he's feeling confident. Danny's a terminal hippie or something, the last person in the world to tamper with a trade secret. Danny could care less. Luck of the Irish. Lester pays the bill.

'Thanks,' says Danny. 'You can have that little case.'

Lester almost offers them money, but that would make it look important. 'Let's go fishing,' he says. 'I've still got a day off.'

'Fishing?'

'I'll buy the beer.'

'Let's buy a trotline!' Danny says. 'I haven't done that in years.'

Lester is surprised. Danny's really excited. 'Aren't they expensive? I thought we'd get a couple cane poles.'

'Yeah! Let's do that too. Come on, man. I probably just made you a fortune. You owe me.'

'A trotline, huh?'

Great, thinks Wendy. Just great.

'We'll need a seine,' explains Danny after they've bought a trotline and enough other line for ten throw lines and two cane poles and a bait bucket and sinkers and corks and a rod and reel and lures and a .22 automatic Winchester and some stink bait. 'We have to seine for bait.'

'Why not some dynamite? And a Hovercraft for those hard-to-reach places?' complains Les. 'Or maybe a spy satellite coded for catfish? Yeah, and some Oriental girls to clean the fish and a psychiatrist and eighty-nine pairs of sunglasses and a few horses and oats and a blowjob artist? You know. Just the necessities.'

'Calm down, Lester. We're still under two hundred.'

'You spent that much in beer.'

'A mistake, I realize. We'll trade four or five cases for some Jack Daniel's.'

Wendy lies on her sleeping bag on a grassy bank above the river and watches three buzzards circle in the sky. She is no longer aware of the sound of the river. She feels warm and lazy. It's nice with the boys gone. There's some sort of tension between Danny and Lester, something she doesn't like. Some macho trip, a competition. They're trying to draw each other out, to prove something. Like Danny's trying to prove that his wishy-washy emotionalism is superior to Lester's cold, hollow logic. And Les is trying to flip it around – show Danny up for a twerp and occasionally flash a little soul himself.

They're on each other's case. And though it's nice they're out fishing, it's so much nicer with just Danny. On this road trip he was actually starting to relax. He's pretty shell-shocked, spooked, however he acts. He's afraid to get too comfortable, he's certain it'll all blow up again.

Probably will.

Mary Ann is floating to the top of the liquid-filled egg again. She's been dreaming of bright jonquil '57 Chevy convertibles and wisteria and the cool, crisp twilights of her one young spring, before the endless guilt crept in, the responsibility. But that's below. Something is pulling her out of the sleeping euphoria. There is a hungry, delicious new feel in her veins, and the angelfish are restive, darting here and there, bumping into the sides of the glass. Schools of bright minnows flutter up her thighs, and there is a persistent darting, winnowing and fluttering, an intense trilling now, almost a high-pitched warble, suddenly birdlike in this strange fluid world. Her body is there, her breath. She gasps. Her chest is heaving. And she's coming.

She wakes to find herself tied to the bed. The room is dark, but there is a presence, a soft presence. A weight at the foot of the bed and that faintly Negro, melodious voice, humming.

'"Yes, sir. That's my baby."'

Chuckles can hear Hugo doing his push-ups, and she smiles. He thinks I'm asleep, she thinks, and Herman's riding him again. She has a champagne hangover and makes a mental note to resist watching the self-improvement videos. There's something weird about those videos, and she has to drink so much to calm down from all the horniness that she's practically hung over all the time. Almost like watching a good skin flick, she thinks, the best ones that play more with your mind, not just meaty stuff. The movie that got her most aroused wasn't even a skin flick. It was by that depressing Swedish guy, Berg something, and had these two chicks in it that looked almost alike, and all one of them did was kiss the other on the shoulder and a chill ran right down Chuckles's back and up her thighs. It was what was going on inside them, she figures, and something in their eyes. Like sometimes just looking at Baby Chili look at Crisco was more exciting than actually watching them make love.

114

Hugo's confused. He was trying to improve her with these videos. She just laughs. Who's educating who?

'Wow, Hugo. Did you just fart?'

Look at him . . . he's pretending he's looking under the bed for something.

'That was Herman,' he mumbles, clinking around some champagne bottles. 'You seen my wallet?'

12

At least this guy likes to do something, thinks Les. He likes fishing and Jack Daniel's and apparently dabbles in pussy from time to time. A hard life. Now me, I work, thinks Les. But not for long, if this video scam pans out. The idea of layered realities had inspired him ever since Vietnam.

Lester had decided to become an aristocrat after waking from a coma in DaNang with so many flies on his lips that he thought he'd grown a mustache. His cot was right next to a window, which was next to the stack of bodies and chunks of bodies they took off returning choppers. The chunks were what got him. He was delirious a lot and was often accompanied by a couple of fantasy bar girls, who showed up when the helicopter sat down. They'd whisper excitedly to each other behind their fans when a severed torso or half a leg hit the ground. 'What a chunk!' they'd giggle. 'Now there's a real chunk.'

Though a homosexual field nurse had been shaving him daily, and he hadn't a hair on his face or anywhere else, both the aristocracy and the mustache notions stuck. He'd noticed that there weren't many rich boys in body bags.

That was lesson one. Lesson two was that God had a real sense of humor.

By the time he'd healed enough to get around Saigon, the scam of sewing heroin into States-bound corpses had become so popular that he felt innovation was called for.

His load made it packed into skulls instead of torsos, and he dug out the eyes of his corpses in San Diego, tugging forth packets of China White.

A week aftger he'd sold his first pound of heroin he and a buddy were playing wild in the streets in San Francisco, doing their James Dean and Jean Paul Belmondo routines, when his buddy went out to sell a gram to a deserving GI. Lester wasn't upset when his friend didn't return immediately, as he was sort of falling in love with this girl who looked like Jean Seberg and laughed like Ingrid Bergman and drove a fancy sports car and, after they made love, asked him never to leave her. But when he finally went to look for his friend, he found him in the alley by the hotel, shot in the mouth. When he got back to the hotel room, the girl and a half pound were gone.

'That's ten grand an inch, slick,' the note read.

He regretted the moment when, with this girl laughing beneath him, he'd remembered a much younger time, when he was in love. He'd thought that love was back, back with money. He'd seen himself beside that girl in her sports car, winding up the hills outside of San Francisco toward their home. Laughing. She was wild. He'd loved that, but the wildness, obviously, could destroy the dream. He smiled. Ten grand an inch. That's rich.

Lester had plenty of junk left, and he sold it. In a couple of months he built his aristocratic façade. You had to be careful. You had to pick your friends, and then you had to out-aloof them.

This aristocracy deal was hardly different from the video concept; what you saw going on on the surface was not what was getting to you underneath. So eleven months out of Vietnam, Lester Darling, masquerading as Jerome W. Mavis II, watched Garrett P. Kennecott III mince across the eighteenth green. Kennecott appeared to be imagining himself as

Ginger Rogers with a cane, skittering sideways down a flight of stage steps.

'Another caddy for the rack,' Kennecott mumbled, sliding the iron into his bag. 'That's two irons he's lost in three months.' His eyes darkened, and sweat popped out on his upper lip. He'd lost the round to Lester by six strokes. 'It's a good thing I thought to count clubs. Can't be too careful.'

'Right.' Lester crushed out his cigarette on the hood of the Rolls. 'We can report him before cocktails.' He was into the driver's seat and started the engine before Kennecott could take his eyes off the little pile of ash smoldering on the silver.

After reporting the caddy they settled by the window of the clubhouse, which overlooked the marina where Kennecott's sloop was anchored. Lester caressed the schooner with lazy eyes while he sipped a Tangueray and soda. Not since the days of the depression had he seen such luxury, such craftsmanship. Not that he had lived through the Great Depression, but he had become acquainted with the quirks of the wealthy by study. A picture book of the great yachts of the late twenties and early thirties was one of his first connections with the world outside Ann Arbor.

Lester tore his eyes from the boat and yawned. 'Ah, here come the ladies,' He rose to greet two blondes in tennis gear, could sense Kennecott's interest and congratulated himself on his selection. They looked classy, and since it had been several days since he'd been with a woman, he had to remind himself that he must also play this scene with a certain disinterest. Though he couldn't really stub out a cigarette on them as he had on the Rolls, he could appear above lust.

This was not easy, for they were tantalizing tidbits. Champagne-cup breasts and long legs keeping tennis skirts almost at eye level.

118

Each gave Lester her hand and kissed him on the cheek.

'Marly, Melissa, this is Garrett P. Kennecott III. Garrett, my tennis partners.' He winked.

'Call me Garrett,' said Kennecott.

'Hi, Garrett.'

'Pleased to meet you, Mr Kennecott.'

Lester leaned back in his chair and watched the girls go to work on Kennecott. They'd just done a season of summer stock and were costing him nine hundred dollars a day – apiece, not counting tips.

Back when Jerome W. Mavis II was just Lester Darling, a kid who quit high school to roughneck in the oil fields, Kennecott was in a Swiss prep school, coddled by tutors, skiing winters and taking his summers on the Riviera. And while Lester was trying to shove a friend's guts back into a cavity from his groin to his brainpan, Kennecott was bickering over the script for a Hasty Pudding musical. Now he was about to get conned.

Lester smiled.

'Then we took off all our clothes and drove the Mercedes into the swimming pool.' Melissa giggled. 'Mavis called it autoeroticism.'

'We auto not a done it,' he said into his drink. These girls deserved a bonus. He winked at Garrett. 'The blessings of wealth are not without their drawbacks. We must put up a good front.'

'If we act serious, can we wiggle out to your sailing craft?' requested Melissa. 'Uncle Nathan's has a nice bar.'

'How about floating out to the wiggle craft?'

'Wiggle to the float?'

'Language.' Kennecott beamed. 'Language.'

The pier and all the boats were shining and immaculate, and Lester had the elevated feeling that he was walking through delicate china. On the East coast was an air of antiquity and grace somehow missing in California. Walking beside Garrett P. Kennecott III, though he sensed an effeteness born of insulation by wealth, he also felt that perhaps it was proper. After all, here he was himself. He, too, deserved a little insulation.

'You'll like Mavis, he's every bit as crazy as you are,' William K. Heinz II, of California, one of Kennecott's classmates, had told him over lunch as they were closing a deal for an industrial park. 'He's great fun.'

Kennecott grinned back at Heinz. 'That would be refreshing,' he allowed.

Most of Lester's new associates didn't know how to have fun. He'd tease them with sublimated hedonism, and soon they'd love him.

'The chain saw is more acceptable than the weenie. Apparently parents would prefer that their children watch a girl chopped and sawed into pieces in great clots of gore than being made love to. Sex today,' observed Mavis across lobster, once they were out to sea, 'is a commodity and a trick. We use it to sell Mazdas and dog food, to trick and trap one another. But that's nothing new. That's the way it's always been. The reason you don't diddle your daddy is because cavemen needed unspoiled goods to trade to allies. Basic politics. It's sugar-coated real estate, and that's what's ingrained in our cultural psyche. Sex is used for security, for trade-offs, and it's veiled with romantic drivel. It's a sales pitch, that drivel. It would change the power structure if people started having fun. If you want to open yourself up for fun, you have to do things that are strange and frightening at first, to break out of the security rut. As long as they have us convinced that happiness is a Rolls-Royce, we're their slaves. Not that there's anything inherently bad about a

120

Rolls. I rather like them. But you can spend all your time trying to get one, and the stuff you have to do to make money is basically deadening, mathematical, uninquisitive. It'll turn you into a robot whether you're making two dollars an hour or a million per quarter. They don't want us to think about the deep things. Dirty movies, for instance, are heavy-handed because we fear and simplify the subject. Yet when could we see ourselves more clearly?'

'Would you like more wine?' purred Melissa. 'Perhaps it will loosen your tongue.'

'With our particular American ingenuity we've managed to externalize the so-called sexual revolution and remain Puritan, acquisitive, cautious, aggressive, mean. Hence the chain saw. We're as adventurous with our emotional lives as lobsters. But such a powerful urge seems to me to beg investigation, to be toyed with till we open the darkness, not treated like a caged alien. Look at us. We're a nation of hype and sales. Four hundred different types of soft drinks. Same cereal, different boxes. People bust their asses all their lives to propagate different packages. Children see other children dancing in ecstasy on TV – all to celebrate different packages. Four thousand times a week. That's what gets 'em off. What a great life. Soft drinks. Cereal. Violence. The investigation of the psychosensual world would necessitate – '

'Try this.' Marly slung a lobster at his head. 'Suck on that.'

Lester caught the lobster and sucked on it, took a bite, put it on his plate, stared at it. Tears brimmed his eyes.

'You see,' he whispered, 'it reminds me of Teresa, my nanny in Tanganyika, and the way she used to beat me with squids while she derided Yankee Imperialist Capitalism as I nibbled on her nipples. If I thought of this lobster as merely an object, shut myself off from the emotional underpinnings, the experience would be empty; I would think you wanted

121

to slap me with a lobster. But now I am enriched.' He ducked a crab leg. 'The world is a larger place.'

'Strawberries and cream for dessert,' announced Kennecott. 'And more champagne.'

Marly grabbed Mavis by the neck.

'You facile unicorn,' she growled. 'You whore.'

'Shall we catch some air?' Melissa nabbed a bouncing bottle of champagne. 'While these two chat?'

Marly jerked him back, and they thumped upon the floor in a rain of melted butter, crab, and artichoke. She almost had him pinned, squirming against him, and he noticed he was holding his fork. Kennecott and Melissa scurried up the steps as her teeth closed on his neck. This was not in the plan. Sure, he'd told them to play it off the cuff, but suddenly he could envision himself dead amid the lobster, a torn jugular pumping great crimson squirts across the buttery floor. He dropped the fork. Chairs tumbled as he rolled on top, and suddenly she was no longer biting but sucking, moaning, and drawing him down into a softness laced with laughter. Her tongue was in his ear, and he could see them in a red Fiat, curling up the hills of Tangier, laughing.

From that point on the weekend got crazy. He lost control because he was having fun, and he spent too much time fucking Marly and getting drunk and not acting very aristocratic. He eventually got in such a good mood that he told the truth about his façade and everybody had a great laugh. Especially Kennecott.

But that was the last he ever heard from Kennecott, and the end of his career as an aristocrat. So, Lester reminds himself, looking at Danny happily unloading the fishing gear from the Mustang, remember that you're doing this little fishing thing only to seem like a nice, laid-back guy.

Don't actually start having fun.

* * *

Danny splashes through the clear water. The granite channels seem ghostly, like white whales sleeping beneath the azure tug of the currents. The bottom of this river is a channel in one of the oldest igneous formations on earth. The water has sliced out the softer corridors of the stone, leaving smooth iron ridges that form graceful ledges and sudden pools beneath the steady push of the consistent, moderately moving water. This is the home of the channel cat.

They would fish all night, and in the morning – lying on a cot with the smell of potatoes and catfish frying, with his grandfather bent over the fire sipping cold beer and the first sun cooking the canvas of the tent and the long, hot call of doves – he'd reach over and pick up the .22 and shoot at the buzzards circling overhead. Easy targets. The bullets would hit and bounce off the armor of hard feathers like pebbles as the great birds flopped their wings once, maybe twice, and soared on up into burning blue.

But the great thing about stringing a trotline was the uncertainty of the footing, the mystery of the dark waters in the night. Your tennis shoes would slip on the slick rock, often sliding into unexpected depths. You went along by feel. It was never quite the same, and Danny sees how his life also needs mystery, why routine doesn't work. After Kim and Guido and his momma, and almost facing the death penalty during the Summer of Love, ol' Dan was shaken and felt like he might blow away unless he grabbed on to something, which turned out to be Christine. She was slow and steady and clear like the river, and said she understood when he said he sometimes felt cheated by not having enough lives, enough bodies. She said she felt that way herself.

He felt such a kindredness of spirit that he married her, and it was a few years before he even felt like looking at another girl. By then it was too late. They'd grown too dependent on each other. The dream of having both stability and freedom was gone.

'Go ahead, Danny,' she said. 'I can take it.' Little tears squeezed out of Christine's eyes and down her cheeks. It killed him. He couldn't be honest anymore. And he began to keep things inside, to resent her and his dependence on her. That must be how Lester feels about everything, Danny thinks, he can't let anything out. He can't be dependent on anything. To get out of the Christine dilemma, Danny had finally given up and lied so, as he figured later, that particular shot at freedom was doomed from the get go.

He'd been working construction for five years, and it was growing deadening as he was growing old. He needed an excuse to get back on the real highway. The highway inside his head had dead-ended. He'd bottled up. So he used the excuse of making money to hit the road. (It's the only way we'll be able to afford kids, much less send them to college.) He borrowed three thousand dollars and drove to the Rio Grande and bought weed. Then to the East Coast. The Appalachians. A little stop in Little Rock. Lake of the Woods was nice. Business and more business.

He loved the feeling of the highway stroking by, but sometimes Yanks would call in a load before they could pay for it, and he'd have to hole up in some snowbound shack in New England, strangers too close, his road-spaced nerves jangled. Or Chulapo would call him to the Rio too soon, and he'd have to hang around poor Mexicans who looked like they might kill just for fun or tuna fish, much less the thousands in his boots. And, of course, he had to snort a lot of speed and coke to keep going, and he had to have extra around for new girls, and after about a year the world began to crack.

He'd grown too spooked to involve anyone in his dope

124

running and lived in perpetual fear of narcs. They loved to bust little guys like Danny because there were no repercussions. He couldn't afford protection. One bunch he knew of, based out of New York, gave the cops an eighteen-wheeler full of pot a week, just to let their other loads get through. How do you compete with that? He grew bitter at the kingpins in South America and Mexico and the rich guys in the States who controlled the business. What about the little, deserving guy like Danny? The independent? It wasn't fair.

To relax was a risk, and he did it anonymously. He'd stuff his pockets with money and cocaine and hit ritzy hotels in strange cities and get so coked out that his subconscious would surface, and suddenly, beautiful young women, somehow allied with him in the overthrow of Latin American dictators and Yankee drug kings, would bring him top economic secrets and pounds and pounds of coke and tender, bizarre sex and wear nurses' uniforms, no panties. Sacred and depraved Joan of Arcs who whored their way into the power structure now wanted to help Danny destroy it.

Come, my sisters. Let's exploit those who exploit you. The sexist power mongers. If you're serious, go for the balls. After living under Big Sister's astringent code and praying to God to forgive him for being naked when he changed from his school clothes into his pajamas, all this cheered him.

Waking up with a new woman in the morning was like finding himself in a different country. The people looked at you strangely. You began to see things about yourself you hadn't known. And, of course, it was nice to have all these erotic, adventurous girls somewhat under his control. What wouldn't one of those feisty little dictators who lived in the arrogant shadow of the US give for a beautiful blond slave girl? Huh? Come, my children, come to Danny. So it would go, under the influence, too coke-spooked to leave the room.

He required a couple of days and a couple of confused 'escorts' to burn himself out, and then it was time to go. He'd get a little sleep and hustle some money home to Christine, who never seemed appropriately grateful. Then he'd hit the road again.

In Nashville, without sleep for six days, he found himself in a hotel room with three nymphets, trying to explain the Sun Dance to them. How the Indians wouldn't eat or sleep for six days and nights to burn out their cognitive minds, and how they'd hook thongs in their chest muscles and pull away till the muscles ripped and the pain and the lack of sleep exploded into visions.

This was somehow all related to the sexual marathon he was encouraging with giant piles of white powder, and the girls were willing but, as usual, growing confused. They didn't understand how South America fit into it, nor the holiness of their mission. Finally he spooked and ran and jumped in his truck. Unfortunately he had four hundred pounds of weed in the camper, due in Boston a week before, and near the outskirts of town he realized he was almost out of gas and panicked.

'Relax, dickhead,' said a tiny voice in his head. 'Pull over here.'

It was a run-down Chevron station, virtually abandoned, with a tiny sign that read: SELF SERVICE, PAY IN CAFE. Happy he didn't have to talk to anyone, he hopped out and shoved the nozzle in the gas tank. Then he rummaged around for oil and poured a quart in the engine. Then he stood by and admired the truck.

Maybe I hear voices and talk to myself, he thought, but this pickup is my friend. Maybe things are going too fast, but I'll have this truck bronzed, soon as I get enough money. It looked like a work truck, not a dopemobile. When Danny crossed the checkpoint, he'd have a sack of McDonald's in his lap, ketchup dripping down his shirt, carpentry tools visible. He'd say he was an American with his mouth full.

For some reason he was crying; it was suspicious to be crying in a filling station. He quickly hopped into the truck and jammed the truck into reverse without taking the nozzle out of the tank. When he pulled over the gas pump, the crashing metal sparked and set fire to the gas spreading across the concrete and curling up the hose into his tank. He felt alone in the cage of flames, like he was suddenly, finally, outside of time. He saw Christine washing dishes and grew even lonelier as he dived through the door before the explosion, which, with the aid of the Tennessee winds, eventually scattered molecules of Danny's pickup over Santa Barbara, California, where little bits of pot and pickup drifted on to the incredible bodies of fourteen-year-old beach babies, who had vague notions of sleazing their way into the movie industry. And one morning in Nicaragua, when Anastasio Somoza, the third richest man in the world, appeared on his veranda, a few molecules plopped into his morning coffee.

'Hey, Danny,' says Lester. 'You know why Jesus wasn't born in Mexico?'

'Yes.'

The CIA and KGB are bound to have Lester's video trick already, thinks Danny as they walk down the river to check the lines. They've probably been reconstructing our nervous systems with subliminal effects without our even knowing it. For years. We've all been programmed. Lester was probably programmed to do whatever he's doing. We're doom-de-doom doomed, just as I've always suspected. Only I used to think it was God, the little funster.

Danny is experiencing a delicious thrill of guilt walking around in wet tennis shoes, because Big Sister strictly prohibited wet shoes, although she allowed they were necessary in the river. You might get your foot cut. But you were supposed to take them off as soon as you got back to camp, to keep from catching cold. When it rained during the school year, she'd make him go to school barefoot, so he wouldn't sit around in wet shoes. Now he happily sloshes around in wet tennis shoes whenever he can. He feels great. He wonders if his whole life has been an effort to break through the iron dimensions laid out by that big, strong woman. She believed in hard work. Why? Programmed, obviously. Maybe the whole feminist movement is a capitalist plot to get more people working. More people working means more people paying taxes, which means more money for big booms. Go get 'em, Lester. Go get 'em, girls. That'll fool 'em.

Lester brings the stringer and lets Danny talk him into staying another day to help run the lines. He doesn't know why. He doesn't like the feeling of slowing down. He starts getting too close to himself. It's scary. Gotta keep busy, he thinks. Bet Hugo's pleased, he imagines. Probably thinks he's head of marketing by now.

The water is cool, and he feels his way across the granite bottom of the river toward Danny, who is holding the trotline above his head so Lester can see a big catfish thrashing like a shark. Danny pulls a club out of his pocket. Whap!

'Toss me the stringer. Hold the line up.'

The individual hooks on the stringer are too small to hook the big gills, so Danny runs the whole thing through the fish's big mouth, and then, so as not to risk it regaining consciousness and finning him while he's trying to unhook it, he merely cuts the leader from the main line. This releases a lot of weight, and the line lifts high out of the water, and five more fish flash in the morning sun.

The locusts are starting to buzz. It's a hot sound. Wendy is pot-drowsy, and the cold beer is nice. She rolls over on her stomach and leafs through a *Playboy* she found in Lester's car. Even when posing in provocative positions with their naked sisters and a tennis racket, these girls are sincerely planning to be marine biologists and stewardesses who will enjoy meaningful relationships with bankers in ski resorts. That's quite a philosophy you got there, Hugh, and the house is nice too.

She tosses the magazine aside and picks up the little .22 Danny made Lester buy. Her daddy taught her to shoot when she was a little girl. He'd take her out through the bright oranges to the back of the orchard and set cans up on a log. He taught her how to lie on her stomach and settle herself, elbows rested, and bring the bead into the crotch of the back sight, center it, exhale and slowly, slowly pull the trigger. She was good. She thinks she's good because of her patience, her infatuation with the process, as much as with the result. She could knock down a hundred cans in a row at sixty yards.

She looks around for something to shoot at. There's butterflies. Wrens. Mockingbirds and Mindy the Yorkshire terrier. Scruffling and scraping under a scrub oak is an armadillo. And there're buzzards. She gets up and drags a sack of beer cans toward an outcrop of granite, about forty yards from the camp. You could fry eggs on this rock, she thinks as she lines up the cans. Back at the camp, she picks up a handful of pebbles and tosses one a few feet from the armadillo's head. It stops scrabbling. Looks in the direction of the pebble. She tosses another. It moves in the direction of the sound. She lures it toward her.

When the armadillo is almost in her lap, she becomes aware that she needs another cold beer. Danny's gonna turn me into an alcoholic. She smiles. But maybe I should be a jogger. Wear a tape deck blasting into my brain after working all day. Jog along the street for another two hours, sucking up carbon monoxide. Jog in place at intersections. Go home to check myself in the mirror. Think about work and watch *Miami Vice*. Go to bed. Get up. Work. Jog.

13

Projection booths. Telephone booths. Booth booths. Sometimes David feels he's spent his life in booths. The booth of his non-Negro body. The booth of his limited mind. The booth of other booths. They're on the foul edge of Houston. In the smog booth. After West Texas it's quite noticeable. He'd never been through such emptiness, except after a week or two in the toot booth, when he'd run out and couldn't score immediately. Talk about emptiness. It was awesome. Now he's trying to get back into the Chuckles booth, a booth that opened in all directions. It didn't make sense. Some people never learn, he reasons. He calls Manny.

'Nothing unusual. No cops. I've checked their phone calls at the desk. Nothing. He goes to work, though. Can't tell you about that.'

'Damn.'

'He doesn't look smart enough to do anything. And he looks quite sad.'

'If he's dumb, he might do something stupid.'

'Infallible.'

'How does he go to work?'

Hugo is taking the elevator up from the underground parking lot when a nice-looking fellow in a three-piece and sunglasses stops it between floors, shoves a gun with a silencer in his ribs, puts his fingers to his lips and pats him down thoroughly. Very quietly. He even runs his hands under his shirt, against his skin. Then motions for Hugo to drop his pants, both pairs. Hugo is remembering when he caught the two homosexuals in the San Angelo health club. He won't get in the Jacuzzi anymore, because of the way they'd been sitting, with the little jets of water shooting right up you know where. He's scared. He knew Houston was sick. But this? In his own building? His own elevator? What would Lester say, or his secretary? He could never look her in the eye again. Much less flirt. He's almost sick. What if he could never walk again? Then the guy motions for him to pull his pants up.

'I hear you're fucking my girlfriend, boss. We're going up to the main floor and out the door like polite people. Got it?'

Hugo's got it.

They slide into a tan sedan, driven by what appears to be a small Mexican boy with a baseball cap and butterfly sunglasses.

'Pretty classy winky for a hick like you, huh?' David sneers at him. Then, as though amazed, he says, 'Good God, she's weird. You cinch it.'

Hugo's pissed off. Then blindfolded and shoved to the floor.

'It's a real ugly fish, all right,' says Danny. He's up to his waist in water and down to his waist in moonlight. 'Hardly a fish.' Lester is holding the bait bucket, and Danny is trying to remove a big hook from the saw-toothed snout of an alligator gar. It's a long yellow thing, with jaws half again as long as its body. The hook's lodged in bone. Its big ugly eyes roll back into its skull as Dan tugs and twists on the hook. 'These nasty bastards get upwards of forty pounds. I'm glad this one's little.' It's six pounds anyway, and strong. It slaps Lester's wrist with its tail, and he almost drops the bait bucket. For some reason he's jumpy. Everything's working out too easy. 'What kind of subliminal stuff you working on? Advertising?'

'You could use it for anything, I guess. We're still in the technical stage. Why don't you just cut the hook off? Or cut its head off? There's too many of the ugly things.'

'Don't want to waste the hook.'

'You're not trying to save its life, are you?'

Danny looks at Lester, then holds the fish in front of him and snaps its neck. It twitches morbidly.

'No. I'm not. These things eat perfectly good bass.'

'Sure, Hugo. I'll meet you for lunch.'

There's that sad, desperate tension in Hugo's voice. It's fairly depressing. Chuckles hurts. Hugo reminds her of a big, loyal dog. He reminds her a little of Vernon, her second stepfather, who came and sat at the steps to their apartment nearly every Saturday, through three more stepfathers. For a long time she thought that that was why stepfathers were called stepfathers. After getting divorced, they'd sit on your steps and cry. She could con most of her other stepfathers without feeling bad, because her mother had generally atrocious taste in men, and most were mean. But Vernon was just helpless and sweet, and Chuckles felt sorry for him. He'd worked in a Hamm's warehouse stacking cases of beer, and often he'd let her sit in one of the big boxes they ran up and down the long, rolling conveyers. It was dark and cool in the warehouse, and he and his buddies would roll her back and forth as long as she wanted.

Chuckles wonders if she could talk Hugo into changing his name from Daley to Hugo St Bernard. She probably could. How classy that would be. Mr and Mrs St Bernard. Fantastic. But wait a minute. Mr and Mrs? Holy shit.

'Right, Hugo. And I'll wear my respectable stuff. Ciao.'

She hangs up and laughs. Ciao. He's probably thinking 'chow.' Dog food. It never ends.

Herman smiles.

David looks at Baby Chili sleeping and ponders the nature of evil. Was what Crisco did to her bad? It was, after all, a form of discipline. It was bad for everybody and endangered everybody when Baby Chili did too much coke. But David suspects that Baby Chili sometimes likes the punishment. He'd seen her eyes glaze over and watched her soar way away in her mind in Crisco's big embrace. She liked that helpless feeling, especially when it was coupled with attention and orgasms. Her crying was part of the game. And she loves and fears Crisco. So how do you explain it? Nobody, in the end, gets hurt. It's not like Olander's monkey.

Olander O. had a spider monkey when David first met him. And he got this monkey strung out on smack, which is not one of Chili's problems, except when she wants to come down. Then, actually, it's therapeutic. Helps her stop, puts her to sleep. But when you walked in the door at Olander's place, the first thing that happened was a hairy little arm reached through its cage and grabbed for your throat. 'Eeeech!' screamed the sickly spider monkey while jabbing at the inside of its elbow with its right index finger. 'Eeeech! Eeeech!' Olander and his friends thought this was pretty funny, and they could make it do almost anything for a shot of heroin. It made David kind of sick. Once, when he and Olander were in the back room conducting a little business, Olander forgot to lock the cage, and the monkey escaped into the bathroom and rifled the drawers and found the hypodermic needles. On his way out, David heard what sounded like a baby crying, and peeked in the bathroom door. There was the monkey, lips snarled back in desperation, weeping like a frantic child, jabbing an empty needle clear through its tiny elbow, over and over again, growing woozy in a spreading pool of blood.

Talk about a river of dreams. Mary Ann can no longer tell if she's sleeping or awake. The hum of the air conditioner is sometimes a song and sometimes an ocean. Starfish latch on to her mind. She can hear a snail move in France, but she can't hear Crisco. She can't hear that lovely voice singing: '"Yes, sir. That's my baby."'

She can't feel anything that's happening now either. She's moving into the past, the way wind looks in the sycamores, and instead of that voice she absolutely does not hear or feel, she hears her mother singing.

> 'Sleep, baby, sleep.
> Thy father is watching the sheep.
> Thy mother is rocking the dreamland tree,
> When down falls a little dream on thee.'

So enough is enough, thinks Lester. This Huckleberry Finn shit has got to stop. We are, after all, adults, he thinks, then looks at Danny. One of us anyway. Danny lacks that tension that grown-ups are supposed to have around the eyes. The resigned, nose-to-the-grindstone look of responsible people. Danny couldn't make a child feel guilty. And this is very important, right? How else do we control the world? Guilt, that's how. That's how Spain stole the Americas from the Indians. Sent in the Catholic church. Jesus was a white man, and he died for your worthless red asses. Do you hear? Died. You might as well have killed him yourselves. But he died for you. Now that's love. And what do you do? Fuck around in the forest? But God is forgiving, you lucky creeps. Give us that forest. That'll get you off the hook. Now the gold.

He smiles, thinking about Rudy. Even Rudy knew how to make little kids feel guilty. It was all 'yes, sir' and 'no, sir' when big Rudy was around, even though he was a happy pig when you got him by himself. Too much joy, that guy. But we fixed that.

What are Rudy's rug rats gonna do for food, he wonders, opening a beer. We'll see how the video biz goes, he figures. Then I'll help 'em. We can't have *me* walking around with a bunch of guilt, now can we? Like those friends of my parents who raise their kids progressively. The types that try to be fair and reasonable, they can't see that the kids are turning the guilt thing around on them, middle-class guilt they're too chicken to burn out. They live inside a formula. No kingdom of heaven for them. Nope, he admits, a world of kids would be too sharp to manipulate. People like me need rational adults. They rationalize.

'This must be over forty pounds of fish, Danny,' he says, dumping another pile of catfish guts into the river. The gars tear into the red, moiling mass. 'I'm about fished out.'

'Don't fish, then.'

Danny's sick of fishing himself. Well, not exactly of fishing, just of catching fish. What's he gonna do with all these fish? There's two or three places in town he could drop them off, say hello to some folks. But he doesn't feel like that either. You go to the river to get away from the pressure pot of a small town or, in his case, a big town. Actually, in his case, both towns. He'd grown to love the anonymity of big cities. And whenever he got over-romantic about his past, his childhood, and thought he was nostalgic for it, he'd just ask himself if he could've gotten away in Oatmeal with what he did last Tuesday or last Thursday night in LA. Towns the size of Oatmeal took a dislike to experimenting with different personalities. It made them nervous. They didn't think it was right. Everybody should have one nice personality. A simple one.

You could get simpled and niced to death.

'You got a freezer, Lester?'

The armadillo is right next to Wendy's sleeping bag. These animals are almost blind and hunt insects by sound. So you toss little pebbles that sound like bugs hitting the ground. They're so cute, thinks Wendy, looking at the ugly prehistoric snout, the powerful claws, the mailed tail. They just root around. Danny had showed her one, just before they found the body. And she'd seen one in the zoo. They scurry like windup toys. Danny said that once they got their head and shoulders partway down a hole, even if you had ahold of their tails and pulled as hard as you could, you couldn't pull 'em out. Like people. Like Dead Baby.

After she was abandoned by her first boyfriend, Wendy wasn't too fond of men. But she knew enough to know where bitterness led, and she knew that if you tried to hurt somebody, it generally came back on you. You hurt yourself worse. And, besides that, she liked to cuddle. Maybe she was infantile, but she loved tenderness. She loved to give it and, of course, when she could, receive it. Maybe she was acting out some frustrated maternal thing. Who knows? So what? But when she hung around bars and got picked up, she generally found that tenderness wasn't in vogue right then. It made men feel trapped. And when they tried tenderness, it seemed fake – maybe they wanted it too much – and the morning after, things felt dead and flat. There were hard, cold walls. And most of the girls had this slick attitude, an erotic payback for the times they'd been jilted. Cold and shallow was in. Yet she'd noticed there was, at least on the surface of it, a more tender attraction between girls. That seemed to be what was happening. And that was how she met Dead Baby.

'Hi,' said Dead Baby. She was standing in the Dead Goat Saloon where Wendy was soaking up gin and tonic and the visuals. 'I'm Dead Baby.'

'I'm Wendy.'

'I'm sad.'

'I'm sorry.'

'Men.'

'I know.'

Dead Baby explained she'd been used, but Wendy eventually got her laughing, and they got drunk. Dead Baby was funny. They started going places together. Wendy had had enough dead, flat sex to last her for a while and was tired of looking. She and Dead Baby were like kids. They went for rides. They even went bowling. It was fun. They made jokes about men, and they were making jokes when they met Maacha. Maacha began to protect Dead Baby from men. She liked her girlfriends to flirt with Dead Baby, who was pretty, but she didn't like anything to come of the flirtations. Wendy didn't see her much anymore. It was sad. The last time Wendy saw Dead Baby, she was doing a weimaraner routine at the Dead Goat. Maacha had bought her a collar and a leash, and Dead Baby was obeying commands in the middle of the dance floor. Something was amiss.

The armadillo wanders away.

Now he's ruined it all, thinks Hugo. He's read about kidnappings. They kidnap you. They kidnap your children. They kidnap your wife. They get ransoms from everybody and then chop you up into little pieces and feed you to a swimming pool of piranhas. No evidence. No football for little Hugo. No fun with Chuckles. They'll get her too. And Mary Ann, what sort of silent grave will she go to? What will they do to her first? What have they already done to her? At least he could've saved Chuckles. He could've said, 'No, Chuckles! It's a trick!' But no. They're smart. They know that in the back of his mind he'll be thinking there's still a chance for his family. Why is he so dumb? Why tomatoes? It's because of something. It's got to be.

After the Teflon-coated Grease Filter fiasco, Hugo tightened his jaws and the Candy Apple Octopus whirled. But it didn't require much attention. When he got home from selling Yellow Pages, he had too much time on his hands. He couldn't fish with little Hugo forever, and one day when they were fishing at the lake, when the tgomato was bright and shiny in the sky, he had a fine idea. He'd buy a waterskiing boat, and in the months of long daylight he and the boy would rent diving gear and water-ski rides.

This blended in nicely with his new social life, which consisted mainly of Pappy, who ran a little cantina at the lake, and Virginia, Pappy's beautiful and feebleminded Appalachian girlfriend. Pappy was a mestizo. Also there was Lupe, the ancient tamale maker, who thought she was a *bruja*. It was a step down from the country club, but after what he did to the club's kitchen, he couldn't bring himself to go back. Another problem was that Mary Ann was seeing too much of Lupe.

One potentially stormy day, against his better judgement, he was convinced by a beautiful mother and daughter to take them out diving. By the time the storm hit, the two women had been under fifteen minutes and had not surfaced. When they did surface, if they did, the likelihood of them seeing the little boat from inside a trough of waves was slim.

The big Coca Cola sign on the hotel had probably blown down, he thought, wondering if Mary Ann had battened down the shutters to the dive shop. To come out today had been dumb. But they were Yankees, pretty, with money. It was good PR unless they died. Then he saw the young one, her blond hair mushrooming on the crest of a three-footer. They fished her out and began circling again as she sprawled on the deck, exhausted, skin quivering, too weak to talk. Her mother appeared fifty feet starboard. Hugo shouted and jumped, trying to get her attention, and Jesus, his helper, let go the wheel to grab the girl's tanks, and the boat swung broadside to a swell, knocking Hugo into the lake. By the time they picked the woman up, she'd lost his tanks.

After they docked and the women were gone, Hugo and Jesus sat drying off in his battened-down shop and listened to the wind.

'It'll be a bad one,' said Hugo.

'It is strange,' said Jesus.

'It's strange that Mary Ann battened down the shop.'

'No, Hugo. She is a good woman.'

'Good and quiet.'

'Perhaps she is having an affair.'

Hugo looked at the sparks of fire in the iron bucket. He was glad they'd left little Hugo at home because of the weather. Jesus was strange.

'Why does this mean she's having an affair, Jesus?' Jesus never joked.

'She did it to make you happy. Right?'

'True.'

'Why does she suddenly want you happy?'

'To have an affair.' He couldn't imagine Mary Ann having an affair. 'You're crazy, Jesus. She's forgotten how to do that.'

'I am crazy, Hugo.'

'True.'

'She is a good woman who always battens down the windows.'

140

'She never battens down the windows. Now shut up.' He watched Jesus cringe away to the cot in the corner by the tanks and lie down. Why the hell did he bring that up?

'Take care of this place, Jesus.' He opened the door and went over to the cantina.

'Hugo! You idiot! They said you drowned.'

'Jesus saved me. Give me a brandy.'

'Sure. Hey, Virginia! Come and see! Hugo is back from the fish.' Virginia sidled through the door that led to the shack behind the bar. She was once from Kentucky. Nobody knew how she had ended up with Pappy, and Pappy wouldn't say. He just smiled.

'Bad night, Hugo,' said Pappy, placing the drink on the bar.

'You thought I was dead.'

Hugo drank the brandy and wondered what it would be like to be with Virginia.

'Go away, Virginia. Hugo is no ghost. Take yourself into the back room.' Virginia disappeared during Pappy's laughter, and the vision of her hips beneath the print dress lingered in Hugo's mind.

'Do not feel bad, Hugo. Everybody looks at my old lady like that. Who knows, maybe someday I will give you a little present. Eh? Let you have my little piece of *rubia*.'

'Thanks a lot, I've got one. Sometimes.'

Nobody else came in the bar.

When Hugo pushed open the door to his house, the light was out and no one was home. Mary Ann's at Lupe's, he thought. She got trapped in the storm on the way home.

During a lull in the storm the door opened and Mary Ann pushed in with little Hugo, bowed over the straw bag she'd used ever since taking up with Lupe. She'd also started to cross herself recently, and Hugo could never remember her being religious.

'Well, hello, Mary Ann.'

'I'm sorry. After the shop I went by Lupe's to get bread. Then the storm got too bad.'

'You battened down the windows.'

'Yes. I remembered.'

'Why? Why this time?'

'Because of the storm. Naturally.' Hugo couldn't imagine her having an affair.

'What a storm,' she said. 'The Coca Cola sign blew off the hotel downtown. Lupe says it will be a bad storm.'

This was unusually talkative of her.

'Lupe knows.' Maybe the storm makes her talk, he thought. He tried to remember if she talked during other storms. She could not possibly be having an affair.

'Jesus nearly capsized the boat today.'

'It was a bad day.'

'We were lucky to get back. Pappy thought I'd drowned.'

'Lupe said you would make it.'

'Lupe knows.' The old bat's convinced Mary Ann that she sees other worlds. Frustrated people get religion, or tomatoes. 'Lupe knows everything in the world,' Hugo said. 'And other stuff.'

'Have a drink. I'll fix something. I'm sorry I'm late, but the storm's a pain.'

'Couldn't Lupe part the waters?'

'Hugo. Bad boy. Pray for your soul.'

'I pray for my dinner. Believe me, it doesn't work.'

She hustled into the kitchen. Hugo watched her hard, athletic hips under the skirt and thought about Virginia. Maybe lightning would strike Pappy tonight. What had Pappy done to deserve Virginia? Every man's dream: beautiful, feebleminded and playful. But Hugo, who had worked all his life, ended up with American Gothic. Thanks a lot, God.

He drank some whiskey quickly, nervous about his boat. The storm was building and he couldn't remember if he'd paid his insurance. Perhaps he should check on his boat, he reasoned, and then stop by the cantina.

The water was a wall. Inside he saw Jesus, sitting in the corner. The electricity was out now, and the bar held the eerie glow of the kerosene lamps. Jesus seemed frightened. Pappy tossed Hugo a towel.

'Did your mama never let you play in the rain, Hugo?'

'Give me a drink and a pint of whiskey.'

'*Seguro.*'

'Hey, Jesus. How's the boat?'

'It's good, Hugo. Don't worry.'

'He tells me not to worry.'

'What should he tell you?' asked Pappy. 'He's Jesus.'

'Shut up, Pappy. I can't remember about my insurance.'

'You paid it, Hugo. Virginia took it to the post office for you last week, along with my coupons.' Hugo smiled. Knocked back his drink. He felt better.

'Tell that beautiful girl to come out, so I can thank her properly.'

'Only *I* thank her properly, Hugo. She only likes me to thank her. The new magazines should be here soon. You can thank them.' Pappy got dirty magazines every month. Hugo liked to watch Virginia look at them.

'I'm tired of thanking magazines.'

'Then thank the Lord.'

'Give me another drink, Pappy.'

Jesus sat at the table in the corner, looking at the closed windows, trembling.

'Jesus almost capsized the boat today.'

'He works hard, Hugo. What is your problem today? I know you. You used to like storms. Boom! Flash!'

'I still like storms. But Jesus had a vision. Jesus says Mary

Ann's having an affair. Who's she poking, Jesus? One of
Lupe's spirit dicks?'

'*Hijo.*' Pappy laughed.

Hugo laughed. He felt better to be laughing in the bar with
Pappy. The door opened and Lupe shuffled in. The wind
had gone cold outside, and Hugo felt a severe chill. The old
woman went over to the bar, and it seemed to Hugo she was
looking at him with one eye and he got nervous. Too much
mescaline in college, he figured. All this witch stuff. Jesus.

'A brandy,' she said.

Pappy got her the brandy.

They all sat silently while the storm beat about the
cantina.

'Why don't you let Jesus stay in your house during the
bad weather,' she said. 'He will freeze in the shop.'

'Whatever you say, ancient one. I don't challenge the
spirits.' He winked at Pappy. When she finished the drink,
the old woman left, and Hugo had to help push the door
shut. She was a very frail old lady, and he couldn't figure
how she had made it to the bar. Then, as he was about to
step into the cold, he felt guilty about the wetback.

'Jesus. Come with me. It'll be warm. You can eat with us.'

'I am fine, Hugo. I don't want to come.'

'Come on.'

Inside there was the smell of soup as they closed the door
and changed out of their wet clothes, and Hugo gave Jesus
some dry pants that were too big. He checked on little Hugo,
who was asleep, and had a drink before they ate. He did not
like Jesus sitting there trembling all the way through dinner,
so he kept drinking and was drunk by the end of dinner.

'This is the woman having an affair,' he asked Jesus.
'Would you have an affair with her? Maybe you need an
affair, Jesus.'

'No, Hugo. You know that is not so.'

144

'You want nothing? Impossible. You may not be too swift, but you are still a man. Here, I offer you my wife. Mary Ann. San Angelo's thrill seeker.' Suddenly it seemed a fine idea. He was tired of Mary Ann pulling silence around her like a bathrobe. He was tired of her silent, self-righteous suffering.

'Take off your clothes, Mary Ann. Jesus hungers after you. Lupe says we must be kind.' Mary Ann ran into the other room crying. Jesus sat with his head bowed.

'You are drunk, Hugo,' he said. 'This is not like you.'

'I have to be drunk. I have to be drunk to live all day with you idiots. You're like robots. Now, will you refuse my hospitality? Will you refuse to help her, Jesus?' Hugo was furious, and forgot that Virginia had taken his insurance to the post office. Tomatoes fell like big red raindrops. 'Right now God is smashing my boat, everything I worked for all my life, to support you silent leeches. Pray for my soul, Mary Ann! Pray for my boat! What kind of life is this?' Hugo lurched to his feet and swayed before Jesus but saw Virginia's hips, separated from him by a ghostly veil of hunched and genuflecting Lupes.

He wept.

David just can't stay mad at Hugo. As a matter of fact, he finds him amazing. The last time he saw something like Hugo was on *The Gong Show*. It just proves Chuckles is loony tunes. And now they have two motel rooms. This new one is actually more of a cottage in a series of cottages, so they could drive inside the little carport and unload the big fellow inconspicuously.

Baby Chili's losing it. He takes her toot away. Makes her drink a Scotch and soda. He takes off her butterfly sunglasses and baseball cap and puts her in bed. He feels a great tenderness for her. She is such a child.

'You get some sleep now, dammit. Don't let Crisco catch you like this.'

Baby Chili hopes Crisco doesn't spank her again. Not just yet. Everything's been pretty weird with this kidnapping stuff. Especially since they nabbed the big guy. And she's been hitting the toot too much. She's as wired as a big bug. Catches herself nervously staring at the wall, frozen, jumping out of her skin when the toilet flushes or the refrigerator kicks in. Crisco doesn't like that. Miss Cool. Miss Control. She doesn't like Chili to get jumpy. And sometimes, like now, when she's been bad and overdone the cocaine, instead of just giving her some downers or junk, Crisco'll make her do even more, gigantic lines that make her heart pound like a bomb, and her knees go weak. Then she'll make her stand in one place naked, without moving, while she does things to her. Sometimes they hurt a little. And Crisco will get her to where she's almost coming, and then stop, so she's breathing real hard and begging for it. And sometimes she'll tie her up and have some of her friends fiddle with her, all at the same time. Once she came so much, she fainted. Then, after an eternity of her heart crawling up her throat, she'll get the spanking. And she'll like the spanking. She'll beg for the spanking. She'll beg Crisco to spank her because she knows that after the spanking, Crisco will fix her a nice shot that will make her all warm and fuzzy after the scary, too-much-coke feeling. And she'll be real nice to Crisco.

'Mommy,' she calls her. 'Mommy, mommy.'

14

Lester tells Wendy and Danny he'll keep the fish on ice and freeze them in Houston. Invites them for dinner when they get down. Hits the road with his software case. The world shimmers and spangles. He floats above it. For once the cold, hard logic evanesces. Mr Nice Guy, he thinks, Mr Slick. Mr Nice Slick took the nice people fishing.

He wheels happily into Houston, concrete everywhere, all around him, and screeches into the underground parking lot of his big ol' high rise. He bops into the elevator, pushes the button. Silence. He's rising, up he goes.

The metallic doors slide sumptuously open onto the plush hallway where a seventeenth-century French Colonial table and mirror sit ridiculously against the velvety wallpaper in front of the elevator. It even smells plush, he thinks. And inside, his pretty IBM sits waiting for the software.

'Hello. David? Hi, sweetheart. Your widdle Chuckles has been looking all *over* for you. Naughty boy, where has him been? Playing wid his weenie again?'

'You bitch.'

'Does he feel silly now? The silly boy? All these kid-napped people everywhere? Does he like his new family?'

'Don't do this to me.'

'You did it to yourself, Jack.'

'That's comforting.'

* * *

The past is a bit oppressive, thinks Dan. He grows morose by the river. His dog is gone, and he drives women nuts. Kim's bandaged head floats up from the bottom of the clear river, floating, shimmering. His grandfather hugs the earth. Otto laughs. Christine cries. His pickup makes like the Fourth of July.

Danny wonders if he's got Otto's brains on his conscience. He had sort of gotten him into the business. To a certain extent. Not a lot, but he'd felt weird about it. It made him wonder what he'd done with his life. He'd been trying to buy his freedom, that's what, like everybody else. Trying to buy the kids and wife a good life. And even after Otto blew his head off, Danny wanted to get rich, but this time for the right reasons. He saw the trap. You had to have an ulterior motive, a big purpose, before the fates would smile on you. Danny's job, as he began to see it, was to get rich in order to instruct humanity in the art of having fun. All the rich folks he knew just kept working, buying gobs of crap, or went into some other cautious, dead routine that insured the slavery of the planet.

Inner space was what he'd work on. He had to get rich to show people how to have a good time, how to get into the carnival of their hearts. He'd pioneer pleasure, strip his senses to the subconscious, open his heart. Burn money up instead of piling it up. This was the least he could do for Otto. Otto'd known how to live. He was fun, and Danny would spread the legacy. Good work if you can get it.

Soon he was flying to Nicaragua with Ernest's father and some boat brokers. Lobster brokers. Broker brokers. All veterans of South American enterprise. All zillionaires. His bosses.

Somoza's buddies.

It seemed the old South American dream still hovered in the clouds, but he was trying not to think about smuggling.

He was full of gin and tonic and love as they flew the coast at eight thousand feet, when the props stopped and he dived for the door. Everybody laughed.

He was to build some bungalows on a Caribbean island for Ernest's father, Ferni. He felt ridiculous with his hand on the door handle, yet the white line of beach had become a white expanse and he could see the storm-torn fronds on the palms. Nobody else seemed worried, however, and though he was happy to get out of Texas for a while, he was not interested in stumbling into any severe responsibility or death, more or less the same things to him. The propellers hadn't budged in over two minutes, and the gray-haired jerks were going over papers, chuckling at this and that.

'Let him jump,' someone said.

They all laughed.

They brushed the palm roofs of some huts on Amberguies Key. Then the pilot switched on the props, and everybody laughed again. Then Danny laughed along with them. Things were like that.

They flew into Managua through smoking volcanoes, over a lake of freshwater sharks, into a city destroyed by earthquake. Jagged walls, smoky red sky, surreal desolation. Danny loved it, wondered what he'd done right. Spoken truthfully, he guessed. One drunk night he happened to be honest to a zillionaire's kid, and next thing you know, he's advising Ferni to make an example of the island and get this Somoza character some good press. 'Keep the concrete and casinos off this island,' he recommended, 'and you'll have National Geographic down here writing articles on the Tycoon Environmentalists.'

Ferni grunted. 'That's what I like about you,' he said. 'You're smart.'

Everybody laughed.

It wasn't till they'd landed in Managua and taken off again

for the island that Danny remembered finding Ernest's wallet under Christine's side of the bed the previous morning. He'd been too excited to think about it. Till now. He'd been sent off to La La Land while Ernest stayed home and fucked his wife.

Still, the island was beautiful.

There was a mountain to the north and a lava-rock coast breaking the waves to the south. The rest of the perimeter was palm-lined, bright white beach. A grass airstrip ran up from a cluster of wooden shacks at the pier. There was no asphalt, no concrete, just thatched screen shacks. The only white man he saw ran alongside the plane, tugging at the door.

'Dovey's been here three months,' said Duncan. 'Ferni was supposed to be back in a week.'

When they introduced Danny as the new architect and engineer, everybody laughed. As they climbed into the jeep Raphael spun the plane around, and when Dan saw it fading toward Managua, he got a helpless, sick feeling. There were no other planes on the island. He was abandoned here, probably sentenced to receiving pornographic photos of Ernest and Christine every week, and deep-sixed if he didn't smuggle enough coke.

'Where's Raphael going?' he asked.

'For the whores.'

Everybody laughed as they bounced down the ruts to Dovey's office at the end of the pier.

'One week!' he shrieked.

While Dovey squawked, Ferni dug around in his bag for a bottle, squinting at the thrashing man with his strange little eyes, and told this story about working for the FBI. 'Tapped Roosevelt's phone, that's what. Listened to him set up his own boys by leaking the right information through a suspected informer. Then, when the Germans had slaughtered enough of our guys to thoroughly trust the source, he'd leak the wrong information, nail 'em for a big one.'

'That's patriotism,' he said. 'That's security.'

He handed Dovey the drink, shook his head.

Dovey smiled. 'It's good to see you.'

It seemed they had a lot of business to catch up on, so Dan walked down the pier, enjoying the slush of the water and the smell of the tides, trying not to think about Ferni's security. The island was nice. The people seemed nice. Nobody tried to sell him anything. He sat on the end of the pier, feeling nicely lonely and far away. Suddenly he didn't give a damn about Ernest and Christine. They deserved each other. But why'd she have to fuck his friends? It hurts more, that's why. And then they act superior.

Well, let them have many children like dazed, well-insured robots. Let them buy automobiles for each of their children. Let these automobiles fill their lungs with carbon monoxide and kill their trees. Let them have more children and more cars. Let them think of money and mascara and hair. For Danny has the island. He is at the heart of the earth, the silent love of time.

He walked to the shack for another cocktail. Half-way through his fifth Scotch, as he was uncontrollably thinking about Ernest and Christine in the bedroom *he* built, Raphael came back with the whores.

> O Fido. O Fido. O where have you been?
> Do you think that you're human?
> Do you write with a pen?

Wendy's versifying again. She's drunk and pouring beer down her shirt in the sunlight. The river laps like a dog.

> Dumb Danny is growing quite sad, don't you see?
> He misses his puppy and makes fun of me.

Danny spins around and sails a cow chip at Wendy's head. He doesn't need anyone cheering him up. Some things are sacred. But he can't help seeing Fido up there behind the clouds, sitting at a little doggy desk, wearing a visor and penning letters. Mark Twain looks over his shoulder. 'No, no, Fido. You don't capitalize *fleas*.'

He loves this girl. She also bothers him. He can't take any more iambic pentameter. At least he hasn't felt trapped yet, but it's something he reflexively worries about. Trapped. Maybe I'm trapped by worrying about being trapped, he considers. He waits till she collects herself from ducking the cow patty, goes back to pouring beer on herself, then sneaks up and pins her shoulders to the grassy bank.

'No more poetry!'

'Hey! What if on a winter's night some travelers were wandering around in a bunch of steam not knowing where they were going but always sensing something of the past or present and even feeling like they were part of something else and you were, too, and then, because of the hiccup of a coffee machine, they saw a bunch of little monkeys dragging a big monkey, whom they called Cold Pop, all around the world on a rope for no reason through a bunch of real smart dwarfs who ran around from word to word, and sometimes between words, arguing about words and trying to seem smarter than the other dwarfs until one or two of the little guys picked up a sign with *word* written on it and planted it in front of the monkeys like it was super-important and erased the word *story*, which was written on the back of the sign, and the monkeys agreed it was too cute for words? And what if they agreed there was a dizzy void between the sign and what it meant? And what if they talked about it a lot? I mean, talked and talked and talked and tried to seem even smarter. And then talked about it some more? Then what if a great white horse flew off into a fairy tale? What do you think? Neat, huh?'

'All right, all right. Poetry. Jesus.'

They kiss.

Little Hugo loved the hot clothes, right when they came out of the dryer. Mary Ann would follow him into the bedroom as he bounded happily ahead of her like a big rabbit and hopped onto the bed where she folded them. The game was that he would lie very still, and she would dump the whole basketful of warm clothes on top of him, submerging him beneath a mountain of warmth and softness. He'd giggle insanely and squawk every time she pulled a piece off the pile. They'd have little tugs-of-war. But sometimes he would lie very still, trancelike, off somewhere in his big little head, luxuriating in the warmth. She had the feeling he could play that game all day.

Crisco has loosened the ties on her arms several times, so Mary Ann can hold the little boy, but she keeps her feet tied, and Mary Ann wouldn't try anything anyway. She's never seen her too clearly, but she's felt her. A big, intense girl. Mary Ann's pretty dazed all the time, and happy for it. She doesn't want to be all that aware of what's happening to her. She is rocking in a cradle of sensation. She's dreaming, dreaming, dreaming . . .

The glow of the computer screen excites Lester. It's as if the earth and skies are opening, the darkness parting. He calls up the first file.

> G 246 G 7 G 111 G 2 G WHIZ WEE WEE WOO
> WOO

He grins. Richard, what a guy.

He makes a cup of coffee. It's going to be a long, long day.

'So you see, numb-nuts, I've got you by the danglers.'

David sees. Chuckles is living up to her name. She can barely talk, she's laughing so hard. He almost laughs himself.

'Three counts of kidnapping!' She nearly chokes. 'You fool.' She chuckles like a porcupine.

It hasn't been three minutes since Hugo and Chili got back, computes David. She's got to be in the immediate area, must've seen them come in the door. He hands the gun to Chili, who holds it on Hugo. Chuckles is still chuckling. He breaks out the door at a dead run, looking for phone booths.

Chuckles gets a grip on herself.

Then somebody else does.

Baby Chili feels silly. She is not at all convinced that one or two of these tiny bullets could stop this big fellow, not for long. He's loony lovesick. In the movies these days, people get shot forever and keep stumbling forward or twitching. One twitch from this guy could knock her head off. And the damn gun is heavy. She backs around behind a chair and rests both hands and the gun on the back and tries to look fiercely into Hugo's big, wide eyes. Apparently he's trying to think. It's sad.

'I'll blow you away, dumbfuck,' she squeaks. 'I'll splatter the walls. Drop your pants.' Never has she seen such confusion. As he's unbuckling his belt it slowly occurs to her that he thinks he's going to be molested. 'That's far enough. Leave them around your ankles. Now sit down.'

Hugo sits.

'That's better. Now tighten the belt.'

This is a trick she learned when she first got to the States.

154

It was for tricks. You make 'em drop their pants and lie back, and then, if they start to get rough or weird, you can pull away and they'll trip over their pants. It saved her once. The creep broke his nose on the doorknob. Chuckles is the one that ought to be shot. Everybody could be in severe trouble. And David. And here I am playing Clint Eastwood to a lovesick moose. Because of Chuckles.

'Chuckles has terminal syphilis, big guy. What do you think about that?'

He starts to cry.

This isn't very funny, she thinks, her face pressed against the glass. The phone booth is suddenly quite crowded. She knows it's David. It's that familiar feeling, an actual warmth, just before the paralyzing pressure in her trapezoid. Good old karate Dave. Everything goes numb, limp. Her mother is doing the Lauren Bacall routine, but it's not working. Chuckles has blown it. Darkness.

They scoot right out of Oatmeal, and it's good to be on the road again. Danny didn't see many Oatmealites, Wendy has noticed. What a homecoming. She's got a wee bit of a hangover, and almost everything makes sense. She's not very excited about Houston, and even less excited that Danny dug up Fido, who's now accompanying them in the trunk. What's left of him.

'It's therapy,' said Danny. 'So I'll quit romanticizing him. Plus, he never got to go on any road trips. Sometimes he got that faraway look in his eye – '

'Why are we going to Houston?'

'To see New Orleans.'

'Aha.'

* * *

155

It is a fairly simple, if tedious, process. Lester discovers he will have to build his own lab, and it will take time. Lots of time. There are a lot of things he doesn't yet understand, but then again, there always have been. But he's made it. He's home-free.

No more partners.

David holds Chuckles as though they're in love, one hand on her cheek as she rests her head on his shoulder. He kisses her as he carries her unconscious form across the street. He's forgotten how light she is, she's been so heavy on his mind. How can she do this to him? He feels like a fruitcake. True love, he figures. True fucking love. Lucky me. It's not right, I can't force her to stay. That's wrong. By the time he gets her inside the room he's crying.

'Did you hurt her?' asks Hugo. He's crying too.

'What's with you guys,' inquires Chili. 'Somebody die?'

David takes the gun. 'Go tie him up good, Chili,' he sobs. He can't stop crying.

Chuckles wakes up, and everybody's crying. Except Chili, who's chopping herself a few lines in disgust. She gives Chuckles her coldest look. 'You bitch,' she says.

Chuckles loves it when Chili tries to be mean. She's easy to tease. But Chuckles can't concentrate on Chili. She's puzzled by Hugo's condition. Pants down. Legs tied. Weeping.

'What did you do to him?'

'Gobbled his goober,' quips Chili. 'For three hours. Twelve times. He's sad I stopped.'

'Liar,' says Hugo.

'Shut up,' says David.

'Party time,' says Chuckles. David's crying is a bad sign and out of character. Or maybe he's finally getting some.

Who knows? But the gun makes her uneasy. 'So what are you going to do, clit breath? Shoot us?'

David imagines what a .357 hollow-point bullet would do to Chuckles's saucy little face. It's sickening. The thing about her was her unpredictability, her dickability, her soul. The hollow-point would end that, too, put an end to that uncanny sensitivity and playfulness that went deeper than the skin. Sure she was a whore. A fun one. That made her a person. Or something. Maybe being a fun person made her a good whore. The thing he loved about her was how she set you free. And he was going to trap that? Hah. It was confusing, and he couldn't ponder it much longer. She could read him like a matchbook.

'Let me think on it,' he says. He wants her to worry, at least a little. 'Maybe I'll let Chili snuff you. She did all the driving.'

'Want a toot, Chuckles?' says Chili. 'I'd like you awake for this one.'

'What would you know about awake, Chili? You're about as awake as a salt shaker.'

When she jumps at Chuckles, David has to whack Chili back in her chair. 'Calm down, Chili. Keep it quiet.'

He lets himself cry again. It's easy. And it confuses Chuckles. He's finally confused her. Out of sight.

'Let's make a deal,' she says.

I've got no choice, reasons Hugo. He thinks of Lester, his boss. But what can he do? He'll just play dumb. Not a hard task. Baby Chili is driving him to the La Quinta to pick up the videos he got from Lester's office. It makes him sick. Chuckles wants to show the videos to David. He knows what will happen then, and it makes him sad. He's betraying his boss, maybe company secrets, and they'll still chop everybody up for the piranha swimming pool. He can't figure out what Chuckles is up to. Is she trying to reform these kidnapper maniacs with Lester's self-improvement videos? They certainly haven't reformed her. But maybe that's because he and Chuckles were in love. Again he is sick with fear. Love, he thinks. He was supposed to love Mary Ann. And now she and little Hugo might get killed because of him.

It wasn't fair. He'd worked hard.

15

Lester is wearing his favorite teddy to celebrate. The dreams of a lifetime are culminating in his very apartment. It just goes to show what perseverance and toughness and control and detachment and industry can do, he thinks. It's an expensive teddy, cost a hundred and seventy-five dollars, a milky, lacy thing, formfitting. It used to drive Richard mad.

Lester wasn't exactly completely gay but felt he should inure himself to homosexuality, so he tried it in much the same spirit that he watched the snuff flick over and over until he could do so without vomiting. It was part of his spiritual progression program. You couldn't waste time worrying about homosexuality, either suppressing or expressing it. Everybody was a little queer, so what?

So he got it out in the open. And he knew what some women meant when they talked about feeling used like a piece of liver. It was a humbling experience, but it was also broadening. It put things in perspective. Now he understood women; nobody could say he didn't. He twists the bottle of champagne in its bucket and looks at himself in the mirror. It's a plain fact. He's beautiful and smart.

As he takes from his closet a pair of fluffy bunny slippers and slides them on his feet, he thinks of what he'll do next with the videos. Now he won't have to involve anyone else. Ever again. And it's not just the quadrillions of dollars he's going to make, or even the power. Nope. It's the artistry, the fun. And, strangely enough, he realizes, beneath it all there is the desire to save the world. 'Let's breed again, like we did last summer,' he hums to himself. He begins the Twist, bumps and grinds at his reflection. He is extremely happy as he dances across the room and pours a memorial glass of champagne for Richard, then one for himself.

It'll work any way you want. Say you want to put someone who's *in* the erotic video business *out* of the erotic video business. Why then, you track some disgusting things beneath the skin flicks. Or say you want to ruin or enhance a particular politician's career, then you doctor their tapes accordingly. Starving types beneath papal motorcades or Vanna White kissing construction workers beneath a Dukakis speech. Yes, especially the rushes of sensuality beneath the repressive, the commonplace. This had certainly freed his secretary. He can still see her blouse opening, revealing untouched regions. She smiled a lot more now.

Crisco watches Mary Ann hold the big little boy. It's strange. Why would anyone name a child Hugo? Why not Otis or Sluggo? The woman is beautiful and has a fragile thing about her that just didn't get translated to the kid. But she loves him a lot, Crisco can tell. It's a quiet, spacey love. Mary Ann can go far away in her head. That's nice.

When Crisco was little, she could go far away in her head. It saved her. When her daddy climbed into bed with her, she had to go away in her head. She would close her eyes and pretend he was Maverick or Peter Pan. She would tell herself how all the world was part of itself, no different. It kept him from getting drunk and beating on her mommy and her little sisters.

She guesses Mary Ann feels about the boy like she felt about her little sisters. Like a big soft umbrella to cover them and a tiger to anybody that hurt them. Crisco has to admit that she's a little nervous about this kidnapping stuff. At first David acted like it was a joyride, then everybody got too twisted. It seemed funny to kidnap the pretty lady, like a joke on Chuckles. But in the clear light of morning – well, dumb.

'How you feeling, sugar?' Crisco's sitting behind her, careful not to let Mary Ann get much of a look. She only fooled around with her in the dark, felt her shudder like an amazed child under the effects of the drugs and her flittering tongue. Here was a perfect straight little housewife, probably never felt anything like that before. She smiles.

'Okay,' Mary Ann says.

'Everything's gonna be all right. Don't worry.'

Mary Ann doesn't say anything.

It's quite a vacation for little Hugo. TV all day. Candy. The nice lady took him swimming. And his mom is right there. Always there. All day. All night. Right there. She hugs him more than she ever has. It's a big city. No school. And they're going to see his dad soon.

And go to a movie.

In Austin, Danny and Wendy go to the Hofbrau on Sixth Street for steaks. It's a balmy night, and Danny is filled with nostalgia. There is the right mixture of the south and west in this lovely town, and just enough extra south to be lush. On certain nights the heavens come down to the streets. It's melodious and fragrant, genteel and earthy and bright. He loves it. Tonight is such a night.

'You look far away, Danny.'

'It's because I'm here.'

A hard, athletic man in a faultless blue suit is shouting to an auditorium full of sparkling faces. The television lights are making everyone sweat.

'And the Lord is looking at each and every one of us. Yes, he is. He knows and feels every little quirk of our thoughts. Every emotion. And the Lord is saying we are *failing* him. Yes, brothers. Yes, sisters. *Failing!* The Lord has found us wanting. But does the Lord smite us? No! Not *yet!* The Lord is giving us another chance. One more *tiny* chance! For eternal – I say *eternal* – salvation! The Lord ain't renting the Promised Land. Nope. He's selling. It's yours forever. *If* you can pay the price. The price. Now, brothers and sisters, I want to ask you something. It's a hard, *hard question.* God never said it would be easy. And it's not. *Are we worth it? Huh?* Look deep. And then turn to your right. Look at your brother on your right. That's right. I want everybody to hold the hand of the Lord and the hand of his brother. And *look deep.* No, no. Some of you look to the left. We can't all look to the right and look deep into each other's souls, now can we? *Just grab somebody.* Hold somebody. And look deep into their eyes and ask yourself. Seriously. Is *he* worth it? Is *she* worth it? Are *we* worth it? *Huh? Say yea!* Say a *joyous* yea!'

Hugo looked like a beaten dog, thinks David, when Chuckles made him and Chili take a walk so they could look at these ridiculous videos. This is insane. He acted jealous that they were watching this trash. Something's wrong. And something, he also realizes, is very weird. His grief over Chuckles had taken him beyond horniness. He had become a deep, vacuous ache. Nothing more. But now, as the preacher reaches both hands toward the heavens, as the audience reaches toward the sky, there are the old stirrings. She seems to be made of flesh again, instead of pain. He feels the current of her eyes and sees her seeing herself in his eyes, sees how she arches her breast toward him. He reaches for her.

* * *

162

The gooks have finished with Max, who is staring stupidly at the hole in his groin, blood dripping from his chin. Then he looks up at Les, who is struggling with fear as the grinning Orientals approach, knives in hand.

'It's good, Les!' shouts Max, blood spitting from his mouth. 'It tastes like chicken!'

This time they actually grab Les and are trying to force something into his mouth. But it's hard. Metallic.

'Wake up, cowboy,' says a flat voice. 'You've got some explaining to do.'

The thing in his mouth is a gun. A .357 Magnum.

Lord, Lord, thinks Chuckles. Now we have breaking and entering and armed robbery as well as the old standby, good ol' garden-variety kidnapping. David looks ridiculous with her nylons over his face. This Lester fellow ain't bad-looking, however. Surprised, of course, to wake up sucking on the business end of a pistol. And probably a little embarrassed about his teddy. I wish Hugo could see his boss now. The ol' St Bernard seemed tormented. Betraying his boss, I guess, bothers him. Not to mention me and David watching the videos together. He's not exactly liberated, old Hugo.

'Trade secret, please.' David is trying to sound tough. 'Tell us the video trick or boom-boom.'

'Fuck you.'

Chuckles laughs. 'We beat you to it,' she says. 'You're fucked. And you must've been expecting it. You're sure dressed for it.'

'I'm coming all over the place.'

I like this guy, thinks Chuckles, a lot.

Hugo can't believe Baby Chili. She is so beautiful and so young. But she seems mean sitting there smacking her gum, watching TV, not paying him any attention. He's sick with fright and jealousy. How could Chuckles do that to him? How could he do it to Mary Ann? In his mind the old *bruja*, Lupe, is leaping about in joy and madness. And what are they going to do to Lester? she cackles. What about Lester? It was hard to keep his voice from shaking when he called Lester's secretary and said he wasn't coming to the office. But it was the truth when he said he was sick. He's real sick, helplessly weak. Tomato breath.

If I get the chance, thinks Hugo, I'm gonna break that David guy in half. In quarters. In eighths. Sixteenths. Thirty-seconds. The thought of him on top of Chuckles makes a really deep hurt in his stomach. It helps to think about various ways of beating him up. He'd break his nose for sure, and maybe stick his finger in a light socket. Break some ribs. Stomp his balls.

'Would you quit that,' snaps Chili. 'I'm watching TV.'

Hugo notices he's smacking his fist into the palm of his other hand. How did David get all these girls? It was weird. He wasn't that neat-looking, so he must have a lot of money. Chuckles said he made dirty movies. He wonders if Baby Chili was in the movies. She was even tinier than Chuckles. Wow.

Ferni and the boys flew in a fresh planeload of whores every day, and Danny had never seen anything like the sun going down at latitude seven degrees north either. Half the heavens blazed smooth and red. The blacks made up to a thousand dollars a month diving for lobster, practically a fortune down there, and they spent it having fun.

Danny felt like he'd found home. Mangoes and bananas rotted on the ground, the bugs were few, and Ferni made no demands. Finally he couldn't get drunk enough to enjoy the whores. They were pretty but hard and guarded, not very inventive. He wondered what they did for fun. Count beads? He finally got a screen shack all to himself and luxuriated in some solitude, and at night, with the water lapping and the wind in the palms and the feel of distant ports pressing his dreams, it seemed to him he'd lain on this same screen porch as a child and that those diesels whining down the night asphalt through the Texas hill country had all been headed here, to paradise, just as he'd dreamed.

He drifted into a restless trance. There was a little school-house in the middle of the jungle, where courses were taught in English. He thought about moving down, becoming a member of the sleepy community, smuggling cocaine to buy the little island, next to the bigger one. They'd secede, become a nation, found the Institute for the Research of the Psychoneurological Aspects of Pleasure and Laziness and Dreams. They'd grow hearts – big, strong, adventurous hearts.

Thinking about all the money it would take, he got that sick, helpless feeling again. Boy, was he slow. Every two weeks the plant's diesel freighters went to Cartagena to pick up fuel. Every other day Ferni's shrimp boats went to Texas. No wonder they didn't care what kind of bungalows he built. Security, he thought, thinking of Ferni's sharp little eyes, knowing they could never talk about it. Ferni could never 'know', in case Danny got caught. Ernest would monitor distribution, and Danny was, in fact, the fall guy. 'How's our architect?'

The laughter was getting on his nerves, and he didn't like the way they dressed. Dovey and Duncan both wore white shoes here in paradise. Nothing, obviously, was sacred.

Soaring back to the mainland, they circled the girls from Managua, who were playing in the morning surf. They panicked when they saw the plane leaving.

The boys had another chuckle.

Back in ugly, stinking Managua, Danny told Ferni he needed to buy plumbing and electrical supplies in the States, and then, upset by how excited he was about the possible big bucks, he wandered around the airport. He was afraid he might actually come back with the supplies, and as he grabbed a bite to eat, he reflected on how impolite Third World types can be. Starving to death in front of the café. Weeping on white shoes. It was hard to enjoy your food. But he was nervous. It was hard to make himself laugh.

He gave a begging girl with two emaciated infants twenty dollars, but even that didn't cheer him. It seemed everybody knew him inside out. The zillionaires were way ahead of him. Tempting him with dreams and girls and pretty islands. It was a trap. But what was he supposed to do, work?

Then he saw the monkey. It wrenched up out of a crowd of stuffed mongooses shooting pool and ugly frogs tap-dancing. Its hairy arms reached above its head, long fingers curled as though reaching for a branch in heaven. For a moment Danny thought about the women dancing in the surf, their arms stretched to the vanishing airplane, but then he realized that if he had a brother, it was this monkey. He was staring into his own eyes. There was a bullet hole under the monkey's left nipple, and on his face was a grimace that might have been a smile before his heart exploded, for he'd been stuffed with an erection.

In the slant-shimmered light of the glass-topped curio counter, hidden among crucifixes, big lizards playing Ping-Pong, and toads shaking castenets, Danny's primordial self had twisted through the ages with a message: Reach for the sky and you're dead.

In Matamoros, Raphael took a picture of Danny and the boys all standing under the plane. Someone had placed the monkey on the wing, and he loomed above them like a ghastly, collective soul, streaking to the stars.

Ernest and Danny stayed up all night when he got back, and discussed merging the dream life with the flesh. They said they would become a nation, conceived in anti-industriousness and dedicated to the proposition that all men were created feebleminded. They wouldn't let anyone who seemed religious, ambitious or organized onto the island. Violators would simply be returned to Detroit, sentenced to years of distinguishing between Vegas, Malibus, Mavericks, and Chevelles. When the coffers were empty, they'd rent the island to the Stones for a party. And *National Geographic*, of course, would be down. Yet he still felt like smashing Ernest's earnest little face.

The boats to the island were held up for two weeks, and Danny had too much time to think. When he got the word to go, he got scared. Too much security down there. And when it came to decision making, he had a habit of telling himself that all the information wasn't in yet. Halfway through an ounce of cocaine it occurred to him there might be some clues in New Orleans. The place was full of clues. Fine, twitchy clues. Unparalyzed types. After a few weeks of searching, he got in touch with Ferni. Even through the phone he could feel the sharp little eyes.

He drifted up into the Appalachians, and it wasn't long before the Sandinistas made chutney out of Nicaragua, and smuggling down there grew difficult. While he was away, Christine got rid of him legally and the monkey physically, and in all fairness, the top of the TV was the wrong place for him. But he reminded Danny of something he couldn't quite explain and didn't want to forget. He finally found him in the trunk of an old Impala he'd used to run weed in. Water had seeped in over the winter, and the monkey's stuffing had rotted. Albino pot plants grew out of his snarling mouth and eyes, but he was still reaching for that branch in heaven, and he still had a hard-on.

* * *

'You bringing Fido to dinner?'

Wendy is actually arching her left eyebrow, something he's not seen her do before. Mindy the Yorkshire terrier has been nervous ever since they put Fido in the trunk, and Danny figures this is what is irritating Wendy. She is, perhaps, jealous of Fido. But he doesn't like to see her upset, and it is, he realizes, sort of a dumb thing to do. Which is why he did it. To exaggerate his nostalgia, get rid of it by making a joke of it. But maybe not. Maybe he needs some solid evidence of the past. The real Fido is inside him, of course. But sometimes he feels like he'll blow away, like life never happened. Fido gives him a hold on history, a grip on the earth, a mooring for his hot-air balloon. Wouldn't Big Sister be proud? They are twenty miles out of Houston and dead ringers to hit the five o'clock traffic.

'Fido never liked fish.'

Lester is more than a little upset. Like an idiot, he'd left Richard's floppy disks sitting out, right in front of the screen, and David had called up the files immediately. On top of that, they've got him tied up. And ever since his little experience in Vietnam, he doesn't like being tied up.

'This looks like the secret. Somebody will understand it.'

Lester tries to look unconcerned. 'That's not it,' he mumbles into his gag.

'Of course not,' says Chuckles. She looks fairly grotesque in the nylon stocking. Her eyes are slitted like an Oriental's. She comes over and tweaks his pecker through the teddy. 'Of course not.'

They move into the other room, and he can hear them opening the door.

Then Danny's voice says, 'Happy Halloween.'

'Condo bondage,' explains Chuckles as they finish tying up Danny and Wendy. 'It's how we relax in the evenings.

168

We hit the condos and tie up a few people. You ought to try it sometime. It's a real ego boost. Last night we tied up the mayor and his mistress. They liked it. And I think your friend likes it. Toodle-oo.'

'I do kind of like it, Danny,' Wendy says, after she unhooks her gag on the doorknob and pulls the guys' off with her teeth. 'It makes me feel so vulnerable. You know what I mean? Like I'm not responsible for whatever wonderful, horrible perversions are going to be wreaked upon my personage. It's a sort of freedom, actually. Don't you think? Like after my first boyfriend left, I was pretty depressed and hurled myself upon the impersonal world. But it wasn't too much fun unless I was coked or speeded out. Enough coke made it all detached. Intense, yes, but impersonal. Which was actually kind of nice. No heavy emotional baggage. You could transcend yourself. Speed was better yet. After a couple of days, cognition burns out and your subconscious surfaces and your body tingles . . . weak and open . . . like communion or something . . .'

'That's grand, Wendy. But let's try to get out of this.'

'You're right. There's no one around to molest us.'

'A shame.'

'Don't shout for help,' pleads Les. 'We've got to keep the cops out of this.'

'Fine with me, asshole,' says Dan. 'Too bad Fido wasn't here. He'd've kicked some ass.'

'Cute teddy,' says Wendy.

'That's that,' says Chuckles. 'We're even. I'm free. You've got a brand-new sex scam with the videos. Happy trails.'

David looks at her and smiles sadly. 'I love you,' he says.

'I love you, too, in a way. It's always "in a way", don't you think?'

'I think as little as possible.'

'I know.'

'Couldn't we tie up a few more people? Just for old times' sake? Maybe tie Hugo and Chili together and hang 'em from a lamppost? Please?'

'I hate to be boring, but no. Poor Hugo's suffered enough. Leave him alone. That's part of the deal.'

'Do you love that oaf?'

'In a way.'

Mary Ann hears little Hugo laughing. It's the second time that woman has taken him swimming. She is now able to admit that the woman has been making love to her. And there is nothing she can do about it. Yet somehow everything's going to be all right. She can feel it. She dreams of a jonquil convertible on a young spring night. Lester's driving.

Chuckles looks very seriously into Hugo's eyes. 'Listen, Hugo. A deal's a deal. Right?'

'Right.'

'The kid and old lady are fine. Your boss is fine. The family needs you. I'll come and meet you sometime. But you must be quiet – about all of this. Promise?'

'I promise.'

'Kiss good-bye.'

After Houston, New Orleans sounds a little stultifying. And there'll be too many people there. Danny would be tempted to spread himself too thin, and both he and Wendy need a rest. She's a kindly, jolly person, and he can put up with a titch of claustrophobia for a spell if it shows up. Who knows? All the information isn't in yet. He spins the car around. Big Sister's at his back. Everything is tenuous and fragile. The road shimmers like a song.

They're going to Canada.

* * *

Mary Ann has that faraway look in her eyes as Hugo drives through the hill country. Little Hugo sleeps. It's autumn and the oak trees are turning. Wild ducks fly by.

'Mary Ann,' he says. 'I've got something to tell you.'

Fiction in Paladin

The Businessman: A Tale of Terror £2.95 ☐
Thomas M. Disch
'Each of the sixty short chapters of THE BUSINESSMAN is a *tour de force* of polished, distanced, sly narrative art . . . always the vision of America stays with us: melancholic, subversive and perfectly put . . . In this vision lies the terror of THE BUSINESSMAN'
Times Literary Supplement

'An entertaining nightmare out of Thomas Berger and Stephen King'
Time

Filthy English £2.95 ☐
Jonathan Meades
'Incest and lily-boys, loose livers and ruched red anal compulsives, rape, murder and literary looting . . . Meades tosses off quips, cracks and crossword clues, stirs up the smut and stuffs in the erudition, pokes you in the ribs and prods you in the kidneys (as in Renal, home of Irene and Albert) . . . a delicious treat (full of fruit and nuts) for the vile and filthy mind to savour'
Time Out

Dancing with Mermaids £2.95 ☐
Miles Gibson
'An excellent, imaginative comic tale . . . an original and wholly entertaining fiction . . . extremely funny and curiously touching'
Cosmopolitan

'The impact of the early Ian McEwan or Martin Amis, electrifying, a dazzler'
Financial Times

'It is as if Milk Wood had burst forth with those obscene-looking blossoms one finds in sweaty tropical palm houses . . . murder and mayhem decked out in fantastic and erotic prose'
The Times

To order direct from the publisher just tick the titles you want and fill in the order form. **PF1**

Original Fiction in Paladin

Paper Thin   £2.95 ☐
Philip First
From the author of THE GREAT PERVADER: a wonderfully original
collection of stories about madness, love, passion, violence, sex and
humour.

Don Quixote   £2.95 ☐
Kathy Acker
From the author of BLOOD AND GUTS IN HIGH SCHOOL: a
visionary collage–novel in which Don Quixote is a woman on an
intractable quest; a late twentieth-century LEVIATHAN; a stingingly
powerful and definitely unique novel.

To order direct from the publisher just tick the titles you want
and fill in the order form.   **PF2**

Fiction in Paladin

In the Shadow of the Wind   £2.95   ☐
Anne Hébert
Winner of the Prix Femina
'A bewitching and savage novel . . . there is constant magic in it'
Le Matin

'Beautifully written with great simplicity and originality . . . an
unusual and haunting novel'
London Standard

Love is a Durable Fire   £2.95   ☐
Brian Burland
'Burland has the power to evoke time and place with total authority
. . . compelling . . . the stuff of which real literature is made'
Irish Times

To order direct from the publisher just tick the titles you want
and fill in the order form.

All these books are available at your local bookshop or newsagent, or can be ordered direct from the publisher.

To order direct from the publishers just tick the titles you want and fill in the form below.

Name _____

Address _____

_____

Send to:
Paladin Cash Sales
PO Box 11, Falmouth, Cornwall TR10 9EN.

Please enclose remittance to the value of the cover price plus:

UK 60p for the first book, 25p for the second book plus 15p per copy for each additional book ordered to a maximum charge of £1.90.

BFPO 60p for the first book, 25p for the second book plus 15p per copy for the next 7 books, thereafter 9p per book.

Overseas including Eire £1.25 for the first book, 75p for second book and 28p for each additional book.

_____

Paladin Books reserve the right to show new retail prices on covers, which may differ from those previously advertised in the text or elsewhere.